全民英檢 *初級* 保證班

聽力與口說 題庫

三大特色
- 完全配合英檢試題
- 模擬試題實戰演練
- 掌握英語學習要領

英檢過關 Easy Go！

李淑娟 查爾斯/著

GEPT

五南圖書出版公司 印行

序言

筆者從事多年的英語教育，深覺國人這幾年來的英語能力，
不但沒有明顯的提升，反而有每況愈下的現象。
偶有外國朋友告訴我們，
他們在問路的時候，常要問好幾個人，
才會碰到能用英語清楚交談的人。
這也讓身為英語教學者的我們，
覺得要為國人英語能力的加強再多盡一份心力。

▼

臺灣在國際化的驅動下，
發展出一套國人使用的英語檢定制度。
雖然對於「考試引導學習」的風潮，
學界正反意見不一，
但不可否認的，我們又多了一項英語學習的動力。
在英檢聽說讀寫四技合一的考試型態中，
我們也再次體認到英語的四項能力應是平衡發展，缺一不可。

▼

然而對國人來說，
聽懂英語和開口說英語仍是最大的挑戰。
常有人問：
「為什麼學了好多年的英語，
一遇上外國友人或是必須用英語的時候，
往往聽得霧煞煞，而且完全開不了口？」
有些企業界的朋友，他們的專業素養很好，
可是一旦碰到要用英語表達的時候，
就完全發揮不出來。
有時候連生活基本用語都說得結結巴巴，
這是多麼讓人氣餒的事情！

▼

英語的聽講能力完全要靠平時的練習，
而且這類的練習必須是重複的，持續不斷的。
臺灣並非英語系國家，能說英語的機會有限。

但正因為如此，
更要善用學校、補教界與出版業的資源，
來鍛鍊、加強英語的聽講能力。

▼

其實語言就是一種習慣。
透過細心觀察、不斷模仿、常常複習，進而記憶，
這絕對是必經的過程。
試想我們過去牙牙學語的時候，
不也是先從父母與老師的言語開始去模仿、學講話，
英語的學習也該如此。
尤其國語和英語在語音、腔調方面有很多差異，
更需要多聽，多模仿。
固定收聽、收看適合程度的英語教學節目（開口跟讀最有效哦！），
唱英文歌曲，多看國外的影集、電影，
或是與外籍人士交談，
這些對英語聽講能力的提升，都是大有幫助的。

▼

筆者以多年的教學經驗，
結合英檢考試的發展趨勢，撰寫本書內容，
詳細分析題型，解析重點，並補充相關用語，
希望幫助廣大考生順利通過英檢考試。
殷切期盼能夠貢獻所學，幫助有心學習英語的人更上一層樓。
Practice makes perfect，與大家共勉！

▼

在此感謝書泉出版社所給予的協助，
並且對於能與前輩高志豪老師合作，感到榮幸之至。
本書雖精心編校，但疏漏難免，
尚請老師與讀者不吝賜教！

李淑娟、查爾斯 合序

目 錄
Contents

聽力測驗答題秘訣
Tips for Test-Taking

Tip1： 先看答案選項做預測。

Tip2： 問答題注意句首疑問詞。

Tip3： 注意相似音的字，音越接近越不可能是答案。

Tip4： 全部要作答，不確定則猜，因為錯誤答案不倒扣。

Tip5： 盡量跟上錄音帶或 CD 的速度，不要考慮太久而影響持續作答。

Tip6： 聽力測驗最重要的答題技巧就是永遠向前看；寧可保持早一步看下一題的答案選項，絕對不要去回想前一題選對了沒有！

編者的叮嚀

　　想要聽力測驗成績亮眼，平常練習的時候就要當 *copy cat* 拷貝貓！隨時把聽到的英語，開口複誦；不論是 *listen and repeat* 或是同步跟讀，都是一定要的啦！再加上像追求男/女朋友一樣的熱情和毅力，持續練習，您的英語聽講能力保證超強！加油唄！

聽力部分

Part I

Listening Comprehension

第一章 全民英檢初級聽力測驗題庫第一組試題

第1部分 看圖辨義（Pictures）

本部分共 10 題，請仔細聽每題播出的題目和 A、B、C 三個選項，根據所看到的圖畫選出最相符的答案，並在答案紙上作答。每題只播出一遍，題目及答案選項都不印在測驗本上。

請聽以下範例：

▌ 你會看到

▌ 你會聽到

Q. Please look at the picture. What time is it?

A. It's twenty-four after ten.

B. It's five-fifty.

C. It's ten to five.

【問】請看圖片，現在是幾點？

【答】A. 現在是 10 點 24 分。

B. 現在是 5 點 50 分。

C. 現在是 4 點 50 分。

正確答案為（C），請在答案紙上塗黑作答。

現在開始聽力測驗第一部分。

Question 1

Picture A

Question 2

Picture B

Question 3

Picture C

Picture D

Picture E

Question 7

Picture F

Question 8

Picture G

Picture H

第**2**部分 問答（Question & Response）

本部分共 10 題，請仔細聽每題播出的題目，只播出一遍，再從測驗
本上的 A、B、C 三個選項中選出一個最適合的對應，並在答案紙上
作答。題目不印在測驗本上。

請聽以下範例：

█ 你會聽到

Hi, Betty, how are you today?

█ 你會看到

A. I'm doing my homework.
B. Pretty good. How about you?
C. It's not far from here.

█ 試題中譯

【問】嗨！**Betty**，你今天好嗎？
【答】A. 我正在做功課。
　　　B. 很好啊！你好嗎？
　　　C. 離這裡不遠。

正確答案為（**B**），請在答案紙上塗黑作答。

現在開始聽力測驗第二部分。

Question 11

A. Yes, she's sleeping now.
B. Yes, she's studying in the library.
C. Yes, she's playing tennis.

Question 12

A. It's on the table.
B. The TV is not on now.
C. NBA basketball game.

Question 13

A. Right. He eats a lot.
B. Yes. He is growing a plant.
C. I'm taller than you.

Question 14

A. In 20 minutes, dear.
B. Sorry, I'm late.
C. Every evening.

Question 15

A. It's in the newspaper.
B. It's in my backpack.
C. It's on the show.

Question 16

A. About 400 kilometers.
B. About 5 hours.
C. Train is more comfortable.

Question 17

A. Yes, I listen to the radio.
B. I don't like jazz music.
C. Yes, once a week.

Question 18

A. Pudding, please.
B. I want to bake a pie.
C. Strawberries are in season now.

A. Sure, it's by the window.
B. Sure, it's on the top floor.
C. Sure, it's around the corner.

A. Yes, it is very nice.
B. I don't think so.
C. He isn't smart, either.

第3部分 簡短對話（Short Conversations）

本部分共 10 題，請仔細聽每題播出的一段對話和一個問題，每段對話和問題播出二遍，然後再從測驗本上的 A、B、C 三個選項中選出一個最適合的答案，並在答案紙上作答。對話內容和問題不印在測驗本上。

請聽以下範例：

▌你會聽到

M: Do you have any plans for this weekend, Jenny?

W: Not yet. I'm just thinking about going hiking.

M: It's too hot outside. Why don't you join me to KTV?

W: KTV? Hmm, that sounds fun.

Q: What will Jenny and her friend probably do this weekend?

▌你會看到

A. They will probably go to KTV.

B. They will probably go hiking.

C. They will probably go out to see planes.

（男）**Jenny**，你這個週末有沒有什麼計畫？
（女）還沒有，我只是在考慮去爬山。
（男）外頭太熱了，何不跟我去 **KTV**？
（女）**KTV**？嗯，那聽起來滿好玩的。

【問】**Jenny** 和她的朋友這個週末可能會做什麼？
【答】A. 他們可能去 KTV。
　　　B. 他們可能去爬山。
　　　C. 他們可能去外面看飛機。

正確答案為（**A**），請在答案紙上塗黑作答。

現在開始聽力測驗第三部分。

Question 21

A. In an art supply store.
B. In a furniture store.
C. In a clothing store.

Question 22

A. To study hard.
B. To practice his work.
C. To taste some food.

Question 23

A. A restaurant waiter.
B. A restaurant guest.
C. A salesperson.

Question 24

A. Playing baseball.
B. Cleaning the house.
C. Going out.

Question 25

A. New clothing.
B. Free tickets.
C. A bargain sale.

Question 26

A. Winter.
B. Spring.
C. Fall.

Question 27

A. He is a music teacher.
B. He practices a lot.
C. He is good at playing the piano.

Question 28

A. He didn't do as what he said.
B. He is going to do it tomorrow.
C. He is not honest.

Question 29

A. It's 12:15.
B. It's 11:15.
C. It's 11:45.

Question 30

A. To eat out.
B. To telephone the pizza house.
C. To get takeout from the restaurant.

第一組試題 聽力原文及詳解

第1部分 看圖辨義（Pictures）

Question 1

┃ 試題原文

For Question Number 1, please look at Picture A.
Question Number 1 : What is the weather like?
    A. It's raining and cool.
    B. It's snowing and cold.
    C. It's sunny and warm.

正確答案為（**B**）

┃ 原文中譯

問：天氣如何？
    A. 下雨，天涼。
    B. 下雪，很冷。
    C. 晴天，很暖和。

┃ 試題解析

1. What is the weather like? 是問現在天氣怎麼樣？也可以用未來式談
   氣象預測，例如：What is the weather going to be like this

weekend? 句中的 like 是形容詞用法，指「像⋯⋯」，而不是動詞「喜歡」的意思。

2. 形容天氣時，常常講天候狀況以及氣溫的感覺，例如：sunny and hot 出太陽， 很熱；windy and cool 有風，涼涼的。圖片中下雪，所以選（B）It's snowing and cold.。每天問問自己天氣如何，要用英文回答，自然而然熟悉各種天氣的說法。

Question 2

試題原文

For Question Number 2, please look at Picture B.
Question Number 2 : What do you see in the picture?

　　A. The bus is crowded.

　　B. Some seats are empty.

　　C. They are riding in a taxi.

正確答案為（**B**）

原文中譯

問：在圖片中看到什麼？

　　A. 公車上很擁擠。

　　B. 有些座位是空的。

　　C. 他們是搭乘計程車。

試題解析

1. crowd 指「群眾」，crowded 是「擁擠」的意思，相當於 full of people。
2. 搭乘交通工具，可以說ride in，例如：ride in a bus/car/taxi。圖片中顯然是搭乘公車，而且有些座位是空的 empty，也可以說 not occupied，答案選（B）。

Question 3

試題原文

For Question Number 3, please look at Picture C.
Question Number 3 : What is the woman doing?

    A. She is reading the paper.

    B. She is drinking coffee.

    C. She is writing her paper.

正確答案為（A）

原文中譯

問：這位女士在做什麼？

    A. 她在看報紙。

    B. 她在喝咖啡。

    C. 她在寫報告。

1. 圖片中顯然女士是在看報紙 reading the paper，而不是在喝咖啡 drinking coffee，所以答案選（A）。
2. paper 可以指「紙張、報紙、書面報告」等不同意思。write a paper 是「寫報告」，也可以說 write a report。school paper 是「校刊」，wall paper 是「壁紙」，paper the wall 則是指「貼壁紙」。

Question 4

試題原文

For Question Number 4, please look at Picture D.
Question Number 4 : Where is the plate?
    A. It is above the table.
    B. It is to the right of the glass.
    C. It is between the knife and the fork.

正確答案為（C）

原文中譯

問：盤子在什麼地方？
    A. 在桌子的上方。
    B. 在玻璃杯的右方。
    C. 在刀子和叉子之間。

試題解析

1. 盤子在桌上，但是答案不能選（A），因為 above the table 是指「桌子的上方」，正確說法是 on the table。

2. to the right of something 是指在某物的右側，to the left of something 是在左側。

3. between A and B 表示「在 A 和 B 之間」，可以用於空間、時間、距離、數字等等，所以答案選（C）。

Question 5

試題原文

For Question Number 5 and 6, please look at Picture E.
Question Number 5 : This is Cindy's calendar. When is she going to call Andy?

    A. On Friday.

    B. On Saturday.

    C. On Sunday.

正確答案為（A）

原文中譯

問：這是 **Cindy** 的行事曆，她哪一天要打電話給 **Andy**？

    A. 在星期五。

    B. 在星期六。

    C. 在星期日。

1. calendar 指月曆、日曆或個人行事曆。按行事曆顯示，call Andy 的時間是星期五 Friday，答案選（A）。
2. Monday ～ Friday 稱為 weekdays「週間」，週末是 Saturday 和 Sunday 兩天。英語的星期，每天都有不同的名稱，不像中文那麼簡單地用數字排列，所以一定要每天自我練習，持續一段時間，自然熟練。

Question 6

■ 試題原文

Question Number 6 : Please look at Picture E again. Today is Sunday. What did Cindy do yesterday?

    A. She visited her grandma.

    B. She went shopping with Nancy.

    C. She called Andy.

正確答案為（**B**）

■ 原文中譯

問：今天是星期日，**Cindy** 昨天做了什麼？

    A. 她去探望祖母。

    B. 她和 Nancy 去購物。

    C. 她打電話給 Andy。

試題解析

1. Sunday 的前一天是 Saturday，從行事曆看到的是 go shopping with Nancy，答案選（B）。

2. 常用 go V.+ ing的活動有：慢跑 go jogging、爬山健行 go hiking、滑雪 go skiing、釣魚 go fishing、航行帆船 go sailing 等等。

3. visit 有「拜訪探望、參觀遊覽、正式訪問」等意思。例如：visit a friend 看朋友、visit the museum 參觀博物館、visit three countries in Africa 訪問非洲的三個國家。

Question 7

試題原文

For Question Number 7, please look at Picture F.
Question Number 7 : What is the man doing?
    A. He's working in the rain.
    B. He's waiting for the train.
    C. He's using an umbrella.

正確答案為（C）

原文中譯

問：這位男士在做什麼？
    A. 他在雨中工作。
    B. 他在等火車。
    C. 他撐著傘。

1. 看到有人撐傘，馬上聯想到下雨 rain，如果沒有注意聽，很可能誤答選項（A）。working 和 walking 的發音一定要分清楚，這是一組常考的混淆音。
2. rain 和 train 是另一組常考的混淆音。train 當名詞是「火車」，當動詞則指「訓練」，例如：on-the-job training 就是「在職訓練」。

Question 8

■ 試題原文

For Question Number 8, please look at Picture G.
Question Number 8 : Where are these people?
    A. In the movie theater.
    B. Inside the station.
    C. Outside the stadium.

正確答案為（**A**）

■ 原文中譯

問：這些人在什麼地方？
    A. 在戲院裡。
    B. 在車站裡。
    C. 在體育場外面。

試題解析

1. 圖片中有大螢幕和一些觀眾，顯然是在戲院裡，所以答案選（A）。theater 可以是「戲劇廳」，movie theater 是「電影院」，「歌劇院」稱為 opera house。「電影」可以說 movie，或是 cinema。

2. stadium 指有看台，可以觀看比賽的「體育場」，供人運動的健身房稱為 gym，是 gymnasium 的簡寫。

Question 9

試題原文

For Question Number 9 and 10, please look at Picture H.
Question Number 9 : Who got the best grade on the test?
　　A. Gena did.
　　B. Eddie did.
　　C. Jason did.

正確答案為（**B**）

原文中譯

問：誰的考試成績最好？
　　A. Gena。
　　B. Eddie。
　　C. Jason。

1. 問人：「考試考得好不好？」可以說：「How did you do on the test?」圖中 Eddie 的分數最高，答案當然選（B）。
2. 考試的「成績」可以說 grade，或是 result，學校發的成績單叫做 report card；體育競賽的得分則說 score。

Question 10

■ 試題原文

Question Number 10: Please look at Picture H again.
What is true about the grades?

    A. Jason got 86.

    B. Eddie's grade is worse than Gena's.

    C. Gena did better than Jason.

正確答案為（C）

■ 原文中譯

問：關於分數，哪一個說法正確？

    A. Jason 考了 86 分。

    B. Eddie 的分數比吉娜差。

    C. Gena 考得比傑生好。

試題解析

1. 關於成績，描述正確的只有（C）。

2. 好與壞的比較，分別是 good-better-best；bad-worse-worst。例如：
   That's better than nothing. 表示「聊勝於無」；It's getting worse.
   表示「情況惡化」。

第2部分 問答（Question & Response）

試題原文

Is Alice still preparing for her test tomorrow?
   A. Yes, she's sleeping now.
   B. Yes, she's studying in the library.
   C. Yes, she's playing tennis.

正確答案為（**B**）

原文中譯

問：**Alice** 還在準備明天的考試嗎？
   A. 對，她現在在睡覺。
   B. 對，她現在在圖書館看書。
   C. 對，她現在在打網球。

試題解析

1. 針對問句裡的 preparing for her test，為考試做準備，相對應的應該是唸書，所以答案選（B），studying in the library。

2. 打球的動詞用 play，例如：play basketball 打籃球、play golf 打高爾夫球等等。彈奏樂器也是用 play，但是請記得要加上冠詞，例如：play the piano 彈鋼琴、play the violin 拉小提琴、play the drum 打鼓、play the trumpet 吹小喇叭等等。另外，播放音樂、影帶等，也是用 play，例如：play VCD 播放 VCD。

Question 12

▌ 試題原文

What's on TV tonight?
 A. It's on the table.
 B. The TV is not on now.
 C. NBA basketball game.

正確答案為（**C**）

▌ 原文中譯

問：今天晚上有什麼電視節目？
 A. 在桌上。
 B. 電視現在沒開。
 C. NBA籃球賽。

▌ 試題解析

1. 本題在題目和選項中出現三次 on，意思都不一樣。on 的用法非常多，最常當介系詞用，例如選項（A）的 on the table，在桌上，其他如：on weekend 在週末、talk on the phone 講電話、on sale 大拍賣、on duty 值班、on vacation 度假等等。

2. 大家都知道電器開關上的 on 是「開」，off 是「關」；turn on 或 switch on 是「打開」，turn off 或 switch off 是「關閉」。選項（B）的 The TV is not on now. 表示電視現在沒開。

3. 電視節目的播出和電影上演，都可以說 on，這是形容詞的用法，表示「正在進行中」。某個節目今晚播出，就說 It's on tonight.。這題問：What's on TV tonight? 回答某個節目才正確，答案選（C）。NBA 代表 National Basketball Association。

■ 試題原文

Oh, my! Your younger brother is growing very tall!
 A. Right. He eats a lot.
 B. Yes. He is growing a plant.
 C. I'm taller than you.

正確答案為（**A**）

■ 原文中譯

問：噢，天哪！你弟弟長得好高啊！
 A. 對，他吃很多。
 B. 對，他在種花草。
 C. 我比你高。

■ 試題解析

1. 本題重點在 grow，當它和形容詞一起使用，就有 become「變成」的意思，例如：grow smaller and smaller，變得越來越小。題目中說 grow very tall，而吃得多對應了長高，答案選（A）。
2. grow 也有「種植」的意思，選項（B）的 growing a plant，指「種植花草」。雖然用字相同，但是意思不同，這是聽力測驗中常見的陷阱。

Question 14

試題原文

When will dinner be ready, Mom?
　　A. In 20 minutes, dear.
　　B. Sorry, I'm late.
　　C. Every evening.

正確答案為（**A**）

原文中譯

問：媽，什麼時候可以吃晚餐？
　　A. 寶貝，再 20 分鐘就好了。
　　B. 對不起，我來晚了。
　　C. 每天晚上。

試題解析

1. 本題的疑問詞是 when，問多久可以準備好，對應的一定是時間，所以答案選（A）。請注意 in 20 minutes 的意思是「再過 20 分鐘，20 分鐘到了的時候」，而不是「20 分鐘內」。例如：比賽 5 分鐘後即將開始，可以說 The game will start in 5 minutes.。

Question 15

■ 試題原文

Where is the new CD you bought for me?
> A. It's in the newspaper.
> B. It's in my backpack.
> C. It's on the show.

正確答案為（**B**）

■ 原文中譯

問：你幫我買的 **CD** 在哪裡？
> A. 在報紙上。
> B. 在我的背包裡。
> C. 在節目中。

■ 試題解析

1. 問題是關於放置東西的地點，三個答案選項看似都是地點，但是（A）和（C）都是抽象的地方，只有（B）的 backpack 背包是正確答案。
2. 請注意：某個消息「在報紙上」，要說 in the newspaper，而不是 on the newspaper，因為指的是報紙的內容。

Question 16

試題原文

How long will it take to Kaohsiung（高雄）by train?
    A. About 400 kilometers.
    B. About 5 hours.
    C. Train is more comfortable.

正確答案為（**B**）

原文中譯

問：坐火車到高雄要多久時間？
    A. 大概 400 公里。
    B. 大約 5 個小時。
    C. 火車比較舒服。

試題解析

1. How long will it take to ...? 是問做某件事，或是到某個地方需要花費多少時間，所以答案選（B）。
2. 選項（A）指距離，應該是回應 How far is it? 的答案。

▌試題原文

Do you have music lessons in school?
   A. Yes, I listen to the radio.
   B. I don't like jazz music.
   C. Yes, once a week.

正確答案為（**C**）

▌原文中譯

問：你在學校有音樂課嗎？
   A. 有，我聽收音機。
   B. 我不喜歡爵士樂。
   C. 有，一週一次。

▌試題解析

1. 以 Do you ...? 開頭的問句，大都以 Yes / No 來回應。因為 lesson 和 listen 發音接近，選項（A）容易造成混淆。
2. 中英文頻率的說法正好相反，英文是先說次數，再說時間。例如：twice a day 一天兩次、four times a year 一年四次等等。

Question 18

■ 試題原文

Do you want strawberry pie or pudding for dessert?
　　A. Pudding, please.
　　B. I want to bake a pie.
　　C. Strawberries are in season now.

正確答案為（**A**）

■ 原文中譯

問：你甜點想吃草莓派還是布丁？
　　A. 請給我布丁。
　　B. 我要烤一個餅。
　　C. 草莓現在正盛產。

■ 試題解析

1. 聽到問句中的 or，知道要做選擇，若聽到選項中有提到其中之一，就是最直接的答案了。所以答案應選（A）。

2. 西式餐飲重視飯後甜點，常會問：What do you want for dessert?「你想吃什麼甜點？」例如：pie、cake、pudding、ice cream 等等，都是常見的甜點。

3. season 除了指氣候上的季節，也是球季，或是服飾的一季。in season 表示「當季、正流行」，尤其指農產品盛產。

試題原文

Can you tell me where the MRT station is?
    A. Sure, it's by the window.
    B. Sure, it's on the top floor.
    C. Sure, it's around the corner.

正確答案為（**C**）

原文中譯

問：你可以告訴我捷運車站在哪裡嗎？
    A. 好啊！就在窗邊。
    B. 好啊！就在頂樓。
    C. 好啊！就在轉角。

試題解析

1. 本題問捷運車站在哪裡，三個選項雖都談到地點，但是 by the window 適用於人或物品的擺放地點，on the top floor 應指辦公室或住所的地點，最恰當的答案是（C）。
2. Where is the MRT station? 是直接問句，如果用間接問句，先說：Can you tell me ...? 或是 Do you know ...?，請記得後面的句子不要把 be 動詞移到主詞前面，應該說：... where the MRT station is?。

Question 20

▌試題原文

Nick is a nice guy, isn't he?
　　A. Yes, it is very nice.
　　B. I don't think so.
　　C. He isn't smart, either.

正確答案為（**B**）

▌原文中譯

問：**Nick** 是個好人，對吧?
　　A. 對，它很好。
　　B. 我覺得不是。
　　C. 他也不聰明。

▌試題解析

1. 這一題最要注意的是主詞，既然談的是 Nick，就不能選（A）的 <u>it is</u> very nice.。
2. 本題的問句是附加問句，說話者的意思在前段 Nick is a nice guy 所表達的是肯定意味，而選項（C）的 isn't smart, either「也不……」，並不是適合的對應。
3. I don't think so. 表達對別人的意見、說法不認同，所以答案應選（B）。

第3部分 簡短對話 (Short Conversations)

試題原文

M: Good evening, may I help you?

W: Yes, please. I'm looking for a wool skirt.

M: What color would you like?

W: Bright colors will be fine with me.

Q: Where are these two speakers?

    A. In an art supply store.

    B. In a furniture store.

    C. In a clothing store.

正確答案為（**C**）

原文中譯

男：晚安！我能為您服務嗎？

女：麻煩你，我想找一件羊毛裙。

男：您想要什麼顏色的？

女：亮一點的顏色都可以。

問：這兩個人在什麼地方？

    A. 在美術用品社。

    B. 在家具行。

    C. 在服裝店。

試題解析

1. 有關談話地點的題目，只要聽到關鍵字，就可以立刻決定答案。在此段對話中，我們聽到 wool skirt 羊毛裙，是屬於服飾類的用字，答案當然選（C）。

2. 在購物時，告訴店員：I'm looking for something.，可以快速找到或是請他推薦。有時只是逛逛，當店員問：May I help you? 的時候，也可以回答：I'm just looking. 或是 I'm just browsing，browse 是「瀏覽」的意思，電腦中的瀏覽器就是 browser。

3. bright colors 指「亮度高的顏色」，各種顏色還可以用 dark 和 light 表示深淺，例如：light blue 淺藍色、dark red 暗紅色等等。

Question 22

試題原文

W: Peter, how did you do on your test yesterday?
M: Not good. I didn't prepare well.
W: You're supposed to work harder.
M: I think you're right. I should practice every day.

Q: What does the man plan to do?
    A. To study hard.
    B. To practice his work.
    C. To taste some food.

正確答案為（**A**）

女：你昨天的測驗考的怎麼樣？
男：不太好，我沒有充分準備。
女：你應該要更用功才對。
男：你說得沒錯，我應該要每天練習。

問：這個男士打算怎麼做？
　　A. 用功讀書。
　　B. 練習他的工作。
　　C. 嚐試某樣食物。

■ 試題解析

1. 問別人考試考得好不好，要說：How did you do on the test?。通過考試是 pass the test，考試不及格 fail the test。
2. 對話中，男士覺得自己準備不夠，應該每天練習，因為 Practice makes perfect. 熟能生巧。work hard 和 study hard 都是認真、努力的意思，答案選（A）。
3. be supposed to 表示「應該」，test 和 taste 的發音非常接近，請多留意。

Question 23

■ 試題原文

W: Would you like a drink with your meal, sir?
M: Hmm, what do you have?

W: We have soft drinks, such as coke, 7-up, and iced tea.
　　But I recommend our white wine, it goes very well with
　　fish steak.

M: Well, that sounds good. I'll have a glass, please.

Q: Who is this man?
　　A. A restaurant waiter.
　　B. A restaurant guest.
　　C. A salesperson.

正確答案為（**B**）

■ 原文中譯

女：先生，您要不要來杯飲料搭配餐點？

男：嗯，你們有什麼飲料？

女：我們有無酒精類的，像可樂、汽水、冰茶等。
　　不過，我建議您喝我們的白酒，它搭配魚排非常好。

男：聽起來好像不錯，好，那就請給我一杯。

問：這位男士是什麼人？
　　A. 餐廳服務生。
　　B. 餐廳的客人。
　　C. 銷售員。

■ 試題解析

1. 本題從最前面的兩句，聽到 drink 和 meal，就可以知道這是用餐的
　　對話，由內容可以知道女的是服務生，男的是客人，答案當然選（B）。

2. soft drink 指「無酒精類的飲料」。

3. 在餐廳裡，如果需要服務生的建議，就說："What do you recommend?"。決定要用的菜色，可以用"I'll have ..."或"I'll try ..."來表達。have 和食物連用時，指「吃、喝」，例如：have a steak「吃牛排」、have some beer「喝點啤酒」。

Question 24

▌試題原文

W: Sam, today is Sunday, can you help me clean up the house?

M: Oh, sorry, Mom. I'm going to play baseball with my classmates.

W: Can't you give me a hand before you go out?

M: Oh, all right, but please let me out after lunch.

Q: What will Sam be doing in the morning?
　　A. Playing baseball.
　　B. Cleaning the house.
　　C. Going out.

正確答案為（**B**）

▌原文中譯

女：**Sam**，今天是禮拜天，你可以幫我打掃房子嗎？

男：噢！媽，對不起，我今天要和同學去打棒球。

女：你出去之前就不能先幫幫我嗎？

男：噢！好吧！不過吃完中飯拜託讓我出去。

問：**Sam** 上午中會做什麼？
　　A. 打棒球。
　　B. 打掃房子。
　　C. 外出。

試題解析

1. 對話中提到不同的時間和不同的事情，但是 Sam 最後答應上午幫忙打掃，下午再外出和同學打球，所以答案選（B）。
2. give someone a hand 是「幫忙、協助某人」的意思，好像多給人一隻手，也可以說：lend someone a hand，都等於 help、assist。

Question 25

試題原文

M: Do you mean we can get a 50% discount if we buy two pieces?
W: Exactly, buy one and get one free.
M: Great! I think it's a good opportunity to get some new clothes.
W: Yes. I'm going to buy some outfits for my family, too.

Q: What are the speakers talking about?
　　A. New clothing.
　　B. Free tickets.
　　C. A bargain sale.

正確答案為（**C**）

男：你的意思是說如果我們買兩件，就可以打五折嗎?
女：沒錯，買一送一啊!
男：真好!我想這是添購新衣服的好機會。
女：對啊!我也要幫家人買一些衣服。

問：他們兩個人在討論什麼?
　　A. 新衣服。
　　B. 免費的票。
　　C. 特價廉售。

■ 試題解析

1. 此段對話的關鍵字有 discount 和 buy one and get one free，可以確認談話主題是與拍賣有關，所以答案選（C）。

2. count 是「計算」，加上字首 dis- 變成否定，指「不算的部分」，就是「折扣」。例如：打八折，不算的部分是 20%，所以英文說 20% discount，或是 20% off。 discount 的重音在第一音節時，做名詞用；重音在第二音節時，做動詞用，指「打折」。購物時請賣方算便宜一點，就說：“Can you give me any discount?”。

3. 對話中在拍賣的是衣服，而 outfit 泛指「外衣」，看到朋友或同事穿的衣服滿好看的，可以說：“Hey, nice outfit!” 來讚美他。

Question 26

■ 試題原文

M: Hello, Amanda. Welcome back! How was your vacation?
W: Wonderful! I spent Christmas in Canada.

M: Wow, how exciting! Did you enjoy the snow?
W: Yes. It was pretty cold, but I had great fun.

Q: What time of year did the speakers mention?
　　A. Winter.
　　B. Spring.
　　C. Fall.

正確答案為（**A**）

原文中譯

男：嗨！**Amanda**，歡迎回來！假期過得如何？
女：很棒耶！我到加拿大過聖誕節呢！
男：哇！好過癮哦！你喜歡下雪嗎？
女：喜歡啊！天氣滿冷的，但是我玩得很開心。

問：他們兩個人談到什麼季節？
　　A. 冬天。
　　B. 春天。
　　C. 秋天。

試題解析

1. 這一題問季節，應該是相當容易判斷，從 Christmas、snow 和 cold，都可以輕易地決定答案就是（A）。

2. 度過節日的動詞用 spend，例如很多人喜歡到臺北101過跨年夜，看煙火秀，體驗萬人倒數的歡樂氣氛：spend New Year's Eve at Taipei 101 to watch fireworks and count down together with thousands of people，在現場一定是興奮極了，How exciting! 不是嗎？

3. 表示玩得高興的說法有：enjoy oneself，have a good/great/wonderful time，have fun，have great/lots of fun。

Question 27

試題原文

W: How did you learn to play the violin so well?
M: Little by little, step by step, and finally you can do it well.
W: That's true, but I'm lazy to keep practicing every day.
M: Don't forget that practice makes perfect!

Q: What do we know about the man?
　A. He is a music teacher.
　B. He practices a lot.
　C. He is good at playing the piano.

正確答案為（**B**）

原文中譯

女：你是怎麼學的，能夠把小提琴拉得這麼好？
男：點點滴滴，一步一步來，最後就可以做得很好了！
女：話是沒錯，可是我就是懶得天天練習。
男：你可別忘了，熟能生巧哦！

問：我們對這位男士了解些什麼？
　A. 他是一位音樂老師。
　B. 他經常練習。
　C. 他很會彈鋼琴。

試題解析

1. 這一題即使沒有全部聽懂，運用刪去法也可以找到答案。對話中提到 play the violin，而不是 play the piano，也沒有說是 music teacher，所以非（A）或（C），答案選（B）。

2. little by little、step by step 表示「一點一點、逐步地」，等於 gradually 的意思。keep + Ving 是「一直在……、持續做……」的意思，如：一直在講話 keep talking。凡事要持續練習才會明顯見效，所以要 keep practicing，最終會達到完美，Practice makes perfect! 是至理名言。

3. be good at something 是「擅長於……」的意思。現在社會上常說的「達人」，就是擅長於某件事的專家，He or she must be good at something。相反的就是 be bad at something，例如：我很不會畫畫，英文可以說：I'm bad at drawing.，或是：I'm not good at drawing at all.。

Question 28

試題原文

W: I think we should buy a new coffee table.

M: No. There's only a small problem with its legs.
I can fix it tomorrow.

W: Always tomorrow! You've already said it a thousand times!

M: OK,OK! I really mean it this time!

Q: Why is the woman unhappy about the man?

A. He didn't do as what he said.

B. He is going to do it tomorrow.

C. He is not honest.

正確答案為（**A**）

原文中譯

女：我想我們該買張新的茶几了。

男：不要買，只是桌腳有一點小問題，我明天就把它修好。

女：又是明天！你已經說過一千遍了！

男：好啦！好啦！我這次是說真的！

問：為什麼女士對男士不滿？

    A. 他都沒有照著所說的去做。

    B. 他明天會做。

    C. 他不誠實。

試題解析

1. 通常在客廳會放一張桌子，招待客人喝的飲料可以擺在上面，因為中國人多喝茶就稱之為「茶几」，而英文可千萬不要說成 tea table 哦！他們喝咖啡，當然是 coffee table 囉！其他像中文說的「紅茶」，英文是 black tea；中文說的「紅砂糖」，英文是 brown sugar，這是文化、認知造成的語言差異。

2. 形容次數很多，中英文同樣都有誇張的說法，幾百、幾千，甚至幾萬。a thousand times 或是 a hundred times，都表示 many times、a number of times。

3. 男士光說不練，所以讓女士很不高興，答案選（A）。didn't do as what he said 表示「沒按照所說的去做」。as you wish 是「如你所願」，as you request 是「依你所要求」。

47

Question 29

試題原文

W: Do you have the time, Jerry?

M: It's a quarter to twelve. It's almost lunch time.

W: Thank you. I forgot my watch today.

M: No problem. You always can ask someone to know the time.

Q: What time is it now?
    A. It's 12:15.
    B. It's 11:15.
    C. It's 11:45.

正確答案為（**C**）

原文中譯

女：Jerry，你知道現在幾點嗎？

男：還有 15 分就 12 點，差不多要吃中飯了。

女：謝謝。我今天忘了戴手錶。

男：沒關係，你一定可以找到人問，就知道時間了。

問：現在幾點？
    A. 12 點 15 分。
    B. 11 點 15 分。
    C. 11 點 45 分。

1. 時間的說法很重要，學習英文一定要弄懂。a quarter 原意是「四分之一」，可以指美金的「25分錢」；講時間則是「15分、一刻鐘」。a quarter to twelve 或說 a quarter till twelve，還是直接講 eleven forty-five，都是指「還差一刻就 12 點，11 點 45 分」，答案選（C）。

2. "Do you have the time?" 這一句話常有人誤以為是問：「你有沒有空？」，事實上是問人有沒有戴錶，知不知道現在是什麼時間，它完全等於 "What time is it?"。 "Do you have a minute?"， "Do you have time to ...?" 才是問：「你有沒有空？」。

Question 30

試題原文

W: I don't want to cook tonight. Shall we eat out?
M: Why not? What do you like to have?
W: I feel like pastry. Noodles, pizza, or ...
M: Pizza! Let's order a pizza and we can eat it at home.
W: Good thinking!

Q: What are they going to do next?
    A. To eat out.
    B. To telephone the pizza house.
    C. To get takeout from the restaurant.

正確答案為（**B**）

▌原文中譯

女：我今天晚上不想做飯，我們出去吃好不好？

男：好啊！你想吃什麼?

女：我想吃麵食類的，像麵條啦、披薩、或是……。

男：披薩！我們叫份披薩，可以在家裡吃啊！

女：好主意！

問：他們接下來會做什麼？

　　A. 出去外面吃。

　　B. 打電話給披薩店。

　　C. 去餐廳買外帶。

▌試題解析

1. 對話中聽到兩人最後決定 Let's order a pizza and we can eat it at home.，要訂披薩在家裡吃，接下來當然該打電話叫外送了，答案選（B）。

2. 家裡不開伙的時候，叫外送 delivery service 或是出去吃 eat out 都很方便。自備餐點去郊遊野餐是 go on a picnic，如果帶著炊具、食材到戶外烹煮，稱為 cook-out 或是 cook-off，這是美國人最喜歡的戶外休閒生活之一。

3. 當別人提出一個建議 suggestion，而回答 "Why not?"，就表示贊成的意思；另外 "Good thinking! "、"Good idea! "、"Sounds great! "，也都有同樣的意味。

4. takeout 是指「外帶、外賣的食物」。速食店和咖啡店在客人點餐時，通常會先問："For here or to go?"「內用還是外帶？」。如果要帶走，說出食物名稱，加上 to go 就可以了。例如：「一份漢堡和大杯可樂，帶走。」可說："A hamburger and　a large coke to go, please."。

Notes

第二章 全民英檢初級聽力測驗題庫第二組試題

第1部分 看圖辨義（Pictures）

本部分共 10 題，請仔細聽每題播出的題目和 A、B、C 三個選項，根據所看到的圖畫選出最相符的答案，並在答案紙上作答。每題只播出一遍，題目及答案選項都不印在測驗本上。

請聽以下範例：

| 你會看到

| 你會聽到

Q. Please look at the picture. What time is it?
   A. It's twenty-four after ten.
   B. It's five-fifty.
   C. It's ten to five.

【問】請看圖片，現在是幾點？

【答】A. 現在是 10 點 24 分。

　　　B. 現在是 5 點 50 分。

　　　C. 現在是 4 點 50 分。

正確答案為（**C**），請在答案紙上塗黑作答。

現在開始聽力測驗第一部分。

Question 1

Picture A

Question 2

Picture B

Question 3

Picture C

Picture D

Picture E

Question 6

Picture F

Question 7and 8

Picture G

Picture H

第2部分 問答（Question & Response）

本部分共 10 題，請仔細聽每題播出的題目，只播出一遍，再從測驗本上的 A、B、C 三個選項中選出一個最適合的對應，並在答案紙上作答。題目不印在測驗本上。

請聽以下範例：

你會聽到

Hi, Betty, how are you today?

你會看到

A. I'm doing my homework.
B. Pretty good. How about you?
C. It's not far from here.

試題中譯

【問】嗨！**Betty**，你今天好嗎？
【答】A. 我正在做功課。
　　　B. 很好啊！你好嗎？
　　　C. 離這裡不遠。

正確答案為（**B**），請在答案紙上塗黑作答。

現在開始聽力測驗第二部分。

Question 11

A. Yes, it is a nice party.
B. Of course. How about you?
C. No, it's her birthday.

Question 12

A. To go, please.
B. I don't know where to go.
C. It is very cold in here.

Question 13

A. What's your name?
B. Yes, she can speak English.
C. Sorry, she's not in.

Question 14

A. Thank you. Do you like it?
B. Thank you. I just bought them yesterday.
C. It looks like fun.

Question 15

A. I haven't finished yet.
B. By the end of this month.
C. It's too difficult for me.

Question 16

A. I did, but I'm not sure if he will be here.
B. Nobody is going to.
C. It was a pleasure to meet him.

Question 17

A. It is a good idea.
B. He doesn't need any help.
C. I'd like a city map, please.

Question 18

A. I prefer a window seat.
B. I like it very much.
C. Medium rare, please.

A. She lives downstairs.

B. She failed in her exams.

C. She's been very well.

A. Yes, I've been to Thailand once.

B. It is a wonderful place.

C. Never. I've been dreaming to go.

第**3**部分 簡短對話（Short Conversations）

本部分共 10 題，請仔細聽每題播出的一段對話和一個問題，每段對話和問題播出二遍，然後再從測驗本上的 A、B、C 三個選項中選出一個最適合的答案，並在答案紙上作答。對話內容和問題不印在測驗本上。

請聽以下範例：

| 你會聽到

M: Do you have any plans for this weekend, Jenny?
W: Not yet. I'm just thinking about going hiking.
M: It's too hot outside. Why don't you join me to KTV?
W: KTV? Hmm, that sounds fun.

Q: What will Jenny and her friend probably do this weekend?

| 你會看到

A. They will probably go to KTV.
B. They will probably go hiking.
C. They will probably go out to see planes.

（男）**Jenny**，你這個週末有沒有什麼計畫？

（女）還沒有，我只是在考慮去爬山。

（男）外頭太熱了，何不跟我去 **KTV**？

（女）**KTV**？嗯，那聽起來滿好玩的。

【問】**Jenny** 和她的朋友這個週末可能會做什麼？

【答】A. 他們可能去 KTV。

　　　B. 他們可能去爬山。

　　　C. 他們可能去外面看飛機。

正確答案為（**A**），請在答案紙上塗黑作答。

現在開始聽力測驗第三部分。

Question 21

A. Its price is too high.
B. She doesn't have enough money.
C. It's sold out.

Question 22

A. She agrees with the man.
B. She wants to take the MRT.
C. She thinks that the man should drive.

Question 23

A. He is an eye doctor.
B. He is a dentist.
C. He is a professor.

Question 24

A. It is very hard to do.
B. No one is coming.
C. Because of the bad weather.

Question 25

A. Going home with her.
B. Finding his car key.
C. Helping him all morning.

Question 26

A. The party is funny.
B. Jenny will be very surprised.
C. They will have a good time tomorrow.

A. When Ms. Smith is not busy.
B. When they have nothing to do.
C. They will talk ten minutes later.

A. To help her with some work.
B. To do what he should do for study.
C. To take off his dirty clothes.

A. At the party.
B. On the phone
C. In the restaurant.

A. He is a salesclerk.
B. He is a factory worker.
C. He is a hair stylist.

第二組試題　聽力原文及詳解

第1部分 看圖辨義（Pictures）

Question 1

■ 試題原文

For Question Number 1, please look at Picture A.
Question Number 1 : What is the man?
    A. He is a painter.
    B. He is an office worker.
    C. He is a soldier.

正確答案為（**A**）

．

■ 原文中譯

問：這位男士做什麼工作？
    A. 他是個油漆工人。
    B. 他是個辦公室職員。
    C. 他是個軍人。

■ 試題解析

1. 圖中男士在粉刷，paint 可以指「畫圖、油漆、粉刷」，答案選（A）。
2. office worker 指「在公司上班的人」，若是在工廠工作則是 factory worker，而 laborer 泛指以勞力賺錢的「勞工、勞動者」。

試題原文

For Question Number 2, please look at Picture B.
Question Number 2 : What is between the man and the woman?

    A. A couch.
    B. A table.
    C. A shelf.

正確答案為（**B**）

原文中譯

問：在男士和女士之間有什麼東西？
    A. 一張沙發。
    B. 一張桌子。
    C. 一個層架。

試題解析

1. 此題考物品的相關位置，between A and B 指「在 A 和 B 之間」，從圖片可以知道是一張桌子，答案選（B）。
2. couch 指「長沙發」，可以躺臥，在美國與 sofa 並無嚴格區別。常躺在沙發上看電視的人就被戲稱為 couch potato，大概也因為一邊吃洋芋片吧！單張有扶手的沙發叫 armchair，搖椅是 rocking chair。
3. shelf 是層架，bookshelf 是「書櫥、書架」。

Question 3

█ 試題原文

For Question Number 3, please look at Picture C.
Question Number 3 : Where is the monkey?
   A. In the zoo.
   B. In the cage.
   C. In the box.

正確答案為（**B**）

█ 原文中譯

問：猴子在什麼地方？
   A. 在動物園。
   B. 在籠子裡。
   C. 在盒子裡。

█ 試題解析

1. 猴子被關在籠子裡，不一定是在動物園裡，所以答案選（B），而不是（A）。
2. box 指「箱子、盒子、匣子」等容器，box lunch 是盒裝的午餐、便當，box office 則是戲院、劇場的「售票處、票房」。

For Question Number 4, please look at Picture D.
Question Number 4 : What do you see in the picture?
 A. A truck is moving along the street.
 B. A train is running on the tracks.
 C. A plane is flying across the sky.

正確答案為（**B**）

原文中譯

問：你在圖片中看到什麼？
 A. 一輛卡車沿路行駛。
 B. 一輛火車在鐵軌上行駛。
 C. 一架飛機在天空飛過。

試題解析

1. 本題測驗幾個常見的交通工具和介系詞的用法，圖片中是火車，答案選（B）。
2. 火車行駛可以說 running，鐵軌是 track(s)。track 也是「痕跡」的意思，和 trace 是同義字；另外還指「CD、磁帶上的音軌，賽場的跑道」。

Question 5

試題原文

For Question Number 5, please look at Picture E.
Question Number 5 : What is Lucy doing?

A. She is singing with Chris.

B. She is taking out her cell phone.

C. She is talking on the phone.

正確答案為（**C**）

原文中譯

問：**Lucy** 在做什麼？

A. 她和 Chris 在唱歌。

B. 她拿出她的手機。

C. 她在講電話。

試題解析

1. 圖中 Lucy 在講電話 talking on the phone，不是在唱歌，答案選（C）。

2. 唱歌拿的是「麥克風」microphone，cell phone 是「手機」，也可以說 mobile phone。

3. talking 和 taking 的拼字、發音都很接近，千萬別混淆！

▋ 試題原文

For Question Number 6, please look at Picture F.
Question Number 6 : What is true about these people?
　　A. They both wear dresses.
　　B. The girl is carrying a purse.
　　C. The woman is wearing a hat.

正確答案為（**A**）

▋ 原文中譯

問：關於這兩人，何者敘述正確？
　　A. 他們兩人都穿洋裝。
　　B. 女孩子帶著皮包。
　　C. 婦人戴著帽子。

▋ 試題解析

1. 圖中的婦人帶著皮包，女孩戴著帽子，答案（B）和答案（C）互相錯置，只有（A）是正確的。
2. wear 當動詞，有「穿著、佩戴、塗抹、蓄留、表露」等意思，當名詞是指「服裝」。例如：wear blue jeans 是「穿牛仔褲」，wear a diamond ring 是「戴鑽戒」，wear perfume 是「擦香水」，wear a beard 是「留鬍子」，wear a smile 是「面帶微笑」，ladies wear 是「女裝」，winter wear 是「冬裝」。

Question 7

█ 試題原文

For Questions Number 7 and 8, please look at Picture G.
Question Number 7 : These people are having a party.
What is Carol doing?
    A. She is cutting the cake.
    B. She is singing the "Happy Birthday" song.
    C. She is blowing out the candles.

正確答案為（**C**）

█ 原文中譯

問：這些人在開慶祝派對，**Carol** 在做什麼？
    A. 她在切蛋糕。
    B. 她在唱生日快樂歌。
    C. 她在吹蠟燭。

█ 試題解析

1. 生日宴會中，大家會唱生日快樂歌 sing "Happy Birthday" song，
　 通常邊唱還邊拍手打拍子 clap。唱完歌，壽星 birthday girl/boy 要
　 許願make a wish，吹蠟燭 blow out the candles，再切蛋糕 cut the
　 cake，跟大家分享 share with everyone。而圖中的 Carol 正在吹蠟
　 燭，答案選（C）。
2. 開派對，英文說 have a party，或是 throw a party。

▌試題原文

For Question Number 8 : Please look at Picture G again.
When is Carol's birthday?
   A. On February twenty-three.
   B. On June twenty-third.
   C. On January twenty-third.

正確答案為（**C**）

▌原文中譯

問：**Carol** 的生日是哪一天？
   A. 2月23日。
   B. 6月23日。
   C. 1月23日。

▌試題解析

1. 日曆顯示 Carol 的生日是 1 月 23 日，答案（A）的 February 是 2 月，答案（B）的 June 是 6 月，只有答案（C）的 January twenty-third 是正確的。
2. 日期要用序數的說法，23 日不能說 twenty-three，應該是 twenty-third。每個月的 1 日是 first，2 日是 second，3 日是 third，25 日是 twenty-fifth。

Question 9

∥ 試題原文

For Questions Number 9 and 10, please look at Picture H.
Question Number 9 : What is happening in the picture?

　　A. A dog is running after a man.
　　B. A dog is playing with a toy.
　　C. A man is feeding a duck.

正確答案為（**A**）

∥ 原文中譯

問：圖片中發生什麼狀況？
　　A. 一隻狗追著一個男子。
　　B. 一隻狗在玩著玩具。
　　C. 一個人在餵鴨子。

∥ 試題解析

1. 圖片中有一隻狗追著一個男子，答案（A）A dog is running after a man. 是正確的描述。run after 是「追逐」的意思，也可以說 chase。

2. dog 和 duck 的發音接近，卻是完全不同的動物。

試題原文

For Question Number 10 : Please look at Picture H again. How is the man feeling ?
　　A. He is excited.
　　B. He is scared.
　　C. He is bored.

正確答案為（**B**）

原文中譯

問：這個男子感覺如何？
　　A. 他覺得興奮。
　　B. 他覺得害怕。
　　C. 他覺得無聊。

試題解析

1. 圖中男子的表情，顯然是緊張害怕，所以答案選（B）。be scared 表示「受驚嚇的、害怕的」，常和 at / by 連用，例如：They were scared at/by the strange noise. 他們被奇怪的聲響嚇了一跳。

2. 形容人的情緒的字要用過去分詞，例如：覺得興奮 be excited，覺得無聊 be bored，覺得感興趣 be interested。形容事物的狀況要用現在分詞，例如：令人興奮的 be exciting、令人無趣的 be boring、令人感興趣的 be interesting。

第**2**部分 問答（Question & Response）

Question 11

試題原文

Are you going to Helen's party this Saturday ?
　　A. Yes, it is a nice party.
　　B. Of course. How about you?
　　C. No, it's her birthday.

正確答案為（**B**）

原文中譯

問：你星期六要去參加 **Helen** 的派對嗎？
　　A. 對，那是很好的派對。
　　B. 當然，那你呢？
　　C. 不是，那是她的生日。

試題解析

1. 第二部分要特別注意問題的開頭。這一題問的是："Are you going to ...?" 不是評論派對的好壞，也不是問派對的性質，所以答案選（B）。

2. 回答 "Of course."，"You're right！"，"That's for sure！"，"Definitely." 都是同意或強調肯定的說法。

▌試題原文

A large coke? For here or to go?
　　A. To go, please.
　　B. I don't know where to go.
　　C. It is very cold in here.

正確答案為（**A**）

▌原文中譯

問：大杯可樂嗎？內用還是外帶？
　　A. 外帶。
　　B. 我不知道該去哪裡。
　　C. 這裡面很冷。

▌試題解析

1. 這是在速食店或咖啡店點餐時的對話，"For here or to go?"，「內用還是外帶？」。回答 to go，表示要帶走，所以答案（A）是完全吻合的對應。
2. to go 還可以表示「還要……，還有……」。例如：路程還有 20 分鐘才到 twenty minutes to go，書還有 5 頁才看完 five pages to go，學校還有一年才畢業 one year to go。
3. coke 和 cold 是近似音。

Question 13

試題原文

Hello! May I speak to Ms. Chen, please?
  A. What's your name?
  B. Yes, she can speak English.
  C. Sorry, she's not in.

正確答案為（**C**）

原文中譯

問：哈囉！請找陳小姐聽電話。
  A. 你叫什麼名字？
  B. 是的，她會講英文。
  C. 對不起，她不在。

試題解析

1. "Hello! May I speak to XXX, please?" 是電話用語，「請 XXX 聽電話」的意思。若直接反問 "What's your name?"，很不恰當；說 "Yes, she can speak English." 更是牛頭不對馬嘴，所以適當的對應是答案（C），也可以說 "Sorry, she's out."。

2. 如果要請問來電者是哪位，應該說："Who's calling, please?"

3. speak、tell、say 三個字都有「說、講」的意思，用法不一樣。說某種語言，要用 speak，例如：說法文 speak French，說德文 speak German，說西班牙文 speak Spanish。講故事、講笑話、或是說謊，要用 tell，例如：tell a story、tell a joke、tell a lie。問好、道別時所說的話，要用 say，例如：say hello、say good night、say good-bye。

試題原文

Amy, your earrings look good on you.
    A. Thank you. Do you like it?
    B. Thank you. I just bought them yesterday.
    C. It looks like fun.

正確答案為（**B**）

原文中譯

問：**Amy**，妳戴的耳環很好看。
    A. 謝謝，你喜歡它嗎？
    B. 謝謝，我昨天剛買的。
    C. 看起來很好玩。

試題解析

1. 句中提到耳環 earrings，是複數形，對應的代名詞都該用 them，而不是 it，所以正確答案是（B）。英語名詞單複數的變化，在中文並無區別，請多多留意哦！
2. 要讚美別人的穿著或配戴的東西，可以說 "Your XXX look(s) good on you."，或說 "You look good in XXX."。例如："Your pink dress looks good on you."，或說 "You look good in the pink dress."。
3. 而回應別人的讚美，最得宜的是先說 "Thank you."，可以再加上 "I'm glad you like it/them." 或是 "I like it/them too."，這是適度表現信心又中肯的回應，千萬別以為該謙虛，就說 "Where!Where!"。

Question 15

▌ 試題原文

When will you finish your report, George?
    A. I haven't finished yet.
    B. By the end of this month.
    C. It's too difficult for me.

正確答案為（**B**）

▌ 原文中譯

問：**George**，你什麼時候可以完成報告？
    A. 我還沒完成。
    B. 月底之前
    C. 對我來說太困難。

▌ 試題解析

1. 問句的重點是 When，光說 "I haven't finished yet." 是不夠的；答案（C）則是適合說明未完成的原因，所以答案（B）最恰當。用 by 加上某個時間，表示 no later than，最晚到那個時候。

2. something is too + adj + for someone 表示某件事對某人來說是如何，這是非常實用的句型。例如：To drink and drive is too dangerous for everyone.，酒後開車對所有人來說都很危險。

█ 試題原文

Did anybody tell Bryan about the meeting?
>A. I did, but I'm not sure if he will be here.
>B. Nobody is going to.
>C. It was a pleasure to meet him.

正確答案為（**A**）

█ 原文中譯

問：有沒有人告訴 **Bryan** 開會的事情？
>A. 我說了，但是我不確定他會不會來。
>B. 沒有人要去。
>C. 很高興認識他。

█ 試題解析

1. 對應的句子要注意時間的一致性，所以選答案（A）。
2. 問句中的 meeting 是指「開會」，答案（C）的 meet 是指「認識」。

Question 17

▌試題原文

How can I help you, sir?
    A. It is a good idea.
    B. He doesn't need any help.
    C. I'd like a city map, please.

正確答案為（**C**）

▌原文中譯

問：先生，請問您需要什麼嗎？
    A. 那是個好主意。
    B. 他不需要任何協助。
    C. 我想要一張市區地圖。

▌試題解析

1. "How can I help you, sir/ma'am?" 是服務人員對進門的客人的招呼用語，最可能的對應是客人表達需求，所以答案（C）是適當的選擇。
2. 購買東西的時候，可以向店員說："I'd like something, please."，或是 "I'm looking for something."。如果暫時不需要店員的協助，就說 "No, thank you. I'm just looking."。

■ 試題原文

Where would you like to sit, ma'am?
　　A. I prefer a window seat.
　　B. I like it very much.
　　C. Medium rare, please.

正確答案為（**A**）

■ 原文中譯

問：女士，請問你想要坐在哪裡？
　　A. 我想要靠窗的位子。
　　B. 我非常喜歡。
　　C. 請煎五分熟。

■ 試題解析

1. a window seat 是指「靠窗的座位」，正是回應選位子的答案。如果在飛機上，還有靠走道的座位 aisle seat，中間的座位是 central seat。
2. prefer = like better，prefer A to B 表示「喜歡 A 勝過 B」。
3. "Medium rare, please." 適用於回答 "How would you like your steak?"「牛排要幾分熟？」。全熟是 well-done，半熟是 medium，三分熟是 rare，生的、未煮的則是 raw，例如：生魚片 raw fish，生蠔 raw oyster。

Question 19

試題原文

Why has Tracy been so down recently?

A. She lives downstairs.

B. She failed in her exams.

C. She's been very well.

正確答案為（**B**）

原文中譯

問：**Tracy** 為什麼最近情緒很低落？

A. 她住在樓下。

B. 她考試不及格。

C. 她身體很好。

試題解析

1. 用 down 形容人的時候，是指「情緒低落、意志消沉、健康衰弱」，應該是有不愉快的事情發生，所以答案（C）無法對應，選（B）才正確。另外 down 也可以指「機件當機、生意下滑、景氣差」的意思。

2. pass the test/exam 表示「考試及格」，fail the test/exam 表示「考試不及格、沒過關」。

█ 試題原文

You have been to Disneyland, haven't you?
　　A. Yes, I've been to Thailand once.
　　B. It is a wonderful place.
　　C. Never. I've been dreaming to go.

正確答案為（**C**）

█ 原文中譯

問：你去過迪士尼樂園，對不對？
　　A. 對，我去過泰國一次。
　　B. 那是一個很棒的地方。
　　C. 沒去過，我一直想去。

█ 試題解析

1. 尾問句的句型，還是要先以肯定或否定來回答。選項（A）的地方說
　　錯，選項（B）則答非所問，只有答案（C）是正確的。
2. have been to somewhere 表示「曾經去過……」，have been
　　dreaming to somewhere 表示「一直想去……」。

第3部分 簡短對話（Short Conversations）

Question 21

試題原文

W: Excuse me, I'm looking for a portable CD player. Can you help me?

M: I'm sorry. We're out of portable CD players right now.

W: When will you have them in stock?

M: We will let you know if you leave your name and phone number with us.

Q: Why cannot the woman buy a portable CD player now?
   A. Its price is too high.
   B. She doesn't have enough money.
   C. It's sold out.

正確答案為（**C**）

原文中譯

女：對不起，我想找一台手提 **CD** 音響，你能幫忙嗎？
男：很抱歉，我們現在手提 **CD** 音響缺貨。
女：你們什麼時候會有貨？
男：請你留下姓名、電話，我們會通知您。

問：為什麼女士現在無法買到手提 **CD** 音響？
   A. 價格太高了。
   B. 她沒有足夠的錢。
   C. 貨品賣完了。

1. 現在無法買到手提 CD 音響的關鍵句是：We're out of portable CD players right now. out of something 表示某樣東西沒有了，例如開車時發現沒油了 out of gas；沒現金了 out of cash；沒時間了 out of time。

2. stock 指「存貨」，in stock 表示「有存貨」，out of stock 指「缺貨」。

3. sold out 指「售完、賣光」，所以答案選（C）。

4. 對話中完全未提及價格或金錢，所以答案選項（A）、（B）毋須考慮。

Question 22

試題原文

M: I've been thinking of selling my car.

W: How come? Don't you need a car to get to work?

M: Yes, I do. But it's not easy to find the parking space.

W: That's true. Maybe taking the MRT is a better idea.

Q: What does the woman mean?

    A. She agrees with the man.

    B. She wants to take the MRT.

    C. She thinks that the man should drive.

正確答案為（A）

原文中譯

男：我一直想賣掉我的車子。

女：為什麼？你不是需要開車去上班嗎？

男：是需要，但是停車位很難找。

女：你說得沒錯，也許搭捷運比較好。

問：女士是什麼意思？

    A. 她同意男士的說法。

    B. 她要去搭捷運。

    C. 她認為男士應該開車。

試題解析

1. 女士的意思從 That's true. 可以知道她肯定男士的說法，所以答案選
   （A），agree表示同意。
2. I've been thinking of/about + N/Ving 表示一直想（做）……。
3. How come? = Why? 問「為什麼、怎會這樣」。
4. parking space是「停車位」，也可以說 parking lot。

Question 23

試題原文

M: Can I make an appointment to see Dr. Chang today?

W: What is the problem?

M: I have a very bad toothache.

W: Well, how about three o'clock this afternoon?

Q: Who is Dr. Chang?
   A. He is an eye doctor.
   B. He is a dentist.
   C. He is a professor.

正確答案為（**B**）

■ 原文中譯

男：我今天可以約個時間看張醫師嗎？

女：你是什麼狀況？

男：我牙痛得很厲害。

女：這樣的話，下午 **3** 點可以嗎？

問：張醫師是什麼人？
   A. 他是一位眼科醫師。
   B. 他是一位牙醫。
   C. 他是一位教授。

■ 試題解析

1. 男士說他牙痛：I have a very bad toothache. 可以確認張醫師是一位牙醫，所以答案選（B）。

2. make an appointment 是與人約定時間，多用於業務方面，例如和醫師、律師、客戶、美容院等等。私人約會才說 date。

3. Dr. = doctor 指「醫師、博士」，在大學校園說 doctor 才是稱呼某位教授，所以答案不能選（C）。

Question 24

試題原文

W: The weather report says that it will be rainy tomorrow.

M: Is it going to be raining hard?

W: Probably. A typhoon is coming.

M: Oh, no! We have to cancel our camping this weekend.

Q: Why do they have to cancel their camping plan?

    A. It is very hard to do.

    B. No one is coming.

    C. Because of the bad weather.

正確答案為（**C**）

原文中譯

女：氣象報告說明天會下雨。

男：會下很大嗎？

女：可能會，有颱風要來。

男：噢！慘了！我們得取消週末的露營活動。

問：為什麼他們必須取消露營活動？

    A. 要去做太困難了。

    B. 沒有人要來。

    C. 因為天候不佳。

1. 必須取消露營活動的關鍵句是：A typhoon is coming. 颱風天當然是 bad weather 不能到山裡、海邊去活動，所以答案選（C）。

2. 發生在西太平洋的暴風雨稱為 typhoon，此字來自中文「颱風」。另外，侵襲墨西哥灣一帶和西印度群島的「颶風」則叫 hurricane，像 2005 年中重創美國紐奧良市的 Hurricane Katrina，幾乎讓全市癱瘓。而 tornado 是「龍捲風」，常發生在美國中西部。

3. rain hard = rain heavily 表示下大雨。

Question 25

■ 試題原文

W: Is this your car key, Jonathan?

M: Oh, yes. I've been looking for it all morning. Where did you find it?

W: You left it on my desk.

M: Thanks a million. I don't know how I can go home without it.

Q: What does the man thank the woman for?
   A. Going home with her.
   B. Finding his car key.
   C. Helping him all morning.

正確答案為（**B**）

原文中譯

女：**Jonathan**，這是你的汽車鑰匙嗎？

男：沒錯，我一整個上午都在找，你在哪裡看到的？

女：你放在我辦公桌上。

男：太感謝你了！如果沒鑰匙，我真不知道要怎麼回家。

問：這位男士為什麼要感謝女士？

　　A. 和她一起回家。

　　B. 找到他的汽車鑰匙。

　　C. 整個早上都幫他的忙。

試題解析

1. Thanks a million. 一百萬個謝謝，就是極為感激的意思，比說 Thanks a lot. / Thank you very much. 更多一點。鑰匙很重要，所以感謝女士，答案選（B）。

2. left 是 leave 的過去式，有「離開、遺留」的意思。如果說 left somewhere 表示離開某地，如果說 left something somewhere 表示把東西遺留在某地。You left it on my desk. 就是「你把它放在我辦公桌上。」。另外，left 也指「左邊」，on the left 就是「在左邊」。英文有些常用字，看似簡單，卻有多重意思，一定要從前後文才能確定它的涵義，要多留意哦！

試題原文

W: Do you know tomorrow is Mandy's birthday?

M: Yes, I do. What are you going to do?

W: Jenny and I are going to give her a surprise party.

M: Great! It's going to be a lot of fun.

Q: What does the man mean?

    A. The party is funny.

    B. Jenny will be very surprised.

    C. They will have a good time tomorrow.

正確答案為（**C**）

原文中譯

女：你知道明天是 **Mandy** 的生日嗎？

男：我知道，你有什麼打算？

女：我和 **Jenny** 想幫她辦個驚喜派對。

男：好耶！一定很好玩！

問：男士是什麼意思？

    A. 派對很可笑。

    B. Jenny 會很訝異。

    C. 明天他們會玩得很愉快。

▌試題解析

1. fun 是「樂趣」，It's going to be a lot of fun. 和 have a good time 都表示「會很好玩、很愉快」的意思，所以答案選（C）。

2. funny 指「奇怪的、滑稽的、可笑的」，和 fun 的意思不太一樣，所以答案不能選（A）。例如：He is a funny guy. 表示他可能是一個愛搞笑、行為或是穿著很怪異、或是古怪的人。My stomach feels a little funny. 表示「我的肚子/胃覺得怪怪的，有點不舒服」。

3. birthday 是「生日」，surprise party 是為了給當事人驚喜，而祕密籌備的派對。所以驚喜的人該是 Mandy，而不是 Jenny，不能選（B）。

Question 27

▌試題原文

M: Ms. Smith, can I talk to you for a minute?

W: Sorry, I'm kind of busy right now. Can we talk later?

M: Sure, it's nothing serious.

W: Good. I'll go to your office when I'm done.

Q: **When are they going to talk?**

    A. When Ms. Smith is not busy.

    B. When they have nothing to do.

    C. They will talk ten minutes later.

正確答案為（A）

男：**Smith** 小姐，方便和你談一下嗎？

女：對不起，我現在有點忙，可以待會兒再談嗎？

男：可以啊！不是很要緊的事情。

女：那好，等我忙完了，我會到你的辦公室去。

問：他們什麼時候會談事情？

　　A. 等 Smith 小姐不忙的時候。

　　B. 等他們沒事做的時候。

　　C. 他們 10 分鐘後會談。

1. Smith 小姐說：I'll go to your office when I'm done. 就是等她把手邊的事情做完，不忙的時候再去找男士談，所以答案選（A）。

2. kind of = sort of 表示「有一點、稍微」，後面加形容詞。例如：I'm kind of tired. 是說「我有點累了。」。It's kind of cold in here. 表示「這裡面有點冷。」。

3. serious 可以指「個性嚴肅、態度認真、事情重大、內容正經」等等不同的意思，It's nothing serious. 是說「事情不嚴重」。記得用 nothing、something、anything 的時候，形容詞要放在後面。例如「我喜歡嘗試新事物。」，英文的說法是：I like to try something new.。

Question 28

試題原文

W: David, don't you think you should start doing your homework?

M: Please don't push me so hard, mom!

W: I don't want to, but you always put off until the last minute.

M: All right, I won't do it again. But can I watch TV first?

Q: What does the mother want her son to do?

　　A. To help her with some work.

　　B. To do what he should do for study.

　　C. To take off his dirty clothes.

正確答案為（**B**）

原文中譯

女：**David**，你不覺得你該開始做功課了嗎？

男：媽！別一直催我嘛！

女：我也不想催你，但是你老是拖到最後 **1** 分鐘！

男：好啦！我不會再這樣了。不過，我可以先看一下電視嗎？

問：媽媽要她兒子做什麼？

　　A. 幫她做些事情。

　　B. 做他唸書該做的事。

　　C. 脫掉髒衣服。

1. 媽媽要兒子去做功課 start doing your homework，就是去做唸書該做的事，所以答案選（B）。

2. start + Ving 表示開始去做……，另外還有 begin、keep、finish 等，後面都是使用 Ving。

3. push 是「推、催促」的意思，push hard 指「用力推、強迫」的意思。

4. put off 是「拖延、延期」的意思，take off 是「脫掉、離開、飛機起飛」的意思。

Question 29

| 試題原文

M: Hello, Bangkok Thai Restaurant. How can I help you?

W: I'd like to make a reservation for 6 o'clock tomorrow night.

M: Your name, please. And how large is your party?

W: My name is Shelly Lin. We are a party of four.

M: Yes, a table for four at 6 o'clock tomorrow night. Thank you, Ms. Lin.

Q: Where is this conversation taking place?

    A. At the party.

    B. On the phone

    C. In the restaurant.

正確答案為（B）

原文中譯

男：哈囉！曼谷泰國餐廳，很高興為您服務。
女：我想訂位，明天晚上 **6** 點。
男：請問尊姓大名？一共有幾位？
女：我叫林雪莉，我們有四個人。
男：好的，明天晚上 **6** 點，四位。林小姐，謝謝您。

問：這段對話在什麼場合發生？
　　A. 在宴會上。
　　B. 在電話中。
　　C. 在餐廳裡。

試題解析

1. 這段對話發生的地點，從第一句話就可以知道是電話用語，很容易確定答案是（B）。如果是在餐廳裡面，通常毋需再說餐廳名字。
2. 要定位、訂票，都可以說 ” I'd like to make a reservation for ...”。
3. party = a group of people 基本意思是「一行人、一夥人」，也可以指「聚會、晚會、派對、黨派」。例如：a Christmas party 耶誕晚會、a search party 搜索隊、a political party 政黨。

Question 30

試題原文

M: How do you like these boots?
W: They're in style, but the color is too bright for me.

M: They look good on you, and boots are on sale this week.

W: Well, maybe trying a different color is not a bad idea.

Q: Who is the man?

    A. He is a salesclerk.

    B. He is a factory worker.

    C. He is a hair stylist.

正確答案為（**A**）

原文中譯

男：你覺得這雙靴子怎麼樣？

女：滿流行的款式，可是顏色對我來說太亮了。

男：你穿起來很好看啊！而且這個禮拜靴子在打折。

女：好吧！也許試試不一樣的顏色也不錯。

問：這位男士是什麼人？

    A. 他是銷售員（店員）。

    B. 他是工廠工人。

    C. 他是美髮師。

試題解析

1. 整段對話是在購買鞋子時的交談，而男士說 "How do you like ...?"，顯然是店員詢問，答案選（A）。

2. in style 表示「流行的、時尚的」，和 fashionable、trendy、up-to-date 同義。反義字是 out of style，out-of-date，意思是「不流行的、落伍的」。

第三章　全民英檢初級聽力測驗題庫第三組試題

第**1**部分 看圖辨義（Pictures）

本部分共 10 題，請仔細聽每題播出的題目和 A、B、C 三個選項，根據所看到的圖畫選出最相符的答案，並在答案紙上作答。每題只播出一遍，題目及答案選項都不印在測驗本上。

請聽以下範例：

▌ 你會看到

▌ 你會聽到

Q. Please look at the picture. What time is it?
　　A. It's twenty-four after ten.
　　B. It's five-fifty.
　　C. It's ten to five.

【問】請看圖片，現在是幾點？
【答】A. 現在是 10 點 24 分。
　　　B. 現在是 5 點 50 分。
　　　C. 現在是 4 點 50 分。

正確答案為（ **C** ），請在答案紙上塗黑作答。

現在開始聽力測驗第一部分。

Question 1

Picture A

Question 2

Picture B

Question 3 and 4

Picture C

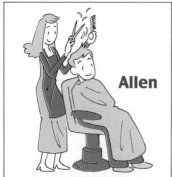

Picture D

Picture E

Question 7

Picture F

Question 8 and 9

Picture G

Picture H

第**2**部分 問答（Question & Response）

本部分共 10 題，請仔細聽每題播出的題目，只播出一遍，再從測驗本上的 A、B、C 三個選項中選出一個最適合的對應，並在答案紙上作答。題目不印在測驗本上。

請聽以下範例：

| 你會聽到

Hi, Betty, how are you today?

| 你會看到

A. I'm doing my homework.
B. Pretty good. How about you?
C. It's not far from here.

| 試題中譯

【問】嗨！**Betty**，你今天好嗎？
【答】A. 我正在做功課。
　　　B. 很好啊！你好嗎？
　　　C. 離這裡不遠。

正確答案為（**B**），請在答案紙上塗黑作答。

現在開始聽力測驗第二部分。

A. Here you are.
B. No problem.
C. No, I'm sorry.

A. Wrap it up, please.
B. Airmail, please.
C. By bus.

A. Yes, medium rare.
B. And a large coke, please.
C. It'll be all right.

A. Nice to meet you.
B. It's far from here.
C. Sure, when is your flight?

Question 15

A. I'm very hungry.
B. This restaurant is very nice.
C. Beef noodles will be fine.

Question 16

A. I like jogging.
B. There is a tennis court nearby.
C. I need to buy running shoes.

Question 17

A. They are on sale.
B. Sorry, I'm late.
C. Oh, when is it?

Question 18

A. Let's eat out.
B. That sounds great!
C. The moon is very beautiful.

A. I moved here last month.

B. I have seen it before.

C. Two or three times a year.

A. There's a post office on the corner.

B. You should watch your steps.

C. It is in the bank.

第3部分 簡短對話（Short Conversations）

本部分共 10 題，請仔細聽每題播出的一段對話和一個問題，每段對話和問題播出二遍，然後再從測驗本上的 A、B、C 三個選項中選出一個最適合的答案，並在答案紙上作答。對話內容和問題不印在測驗本上。

請聽以下範例：

你會聽到

M: Do you have any plans for this weekend, Jenny?
W: Not yet. I'm just thinking about going hiking.
M: It's too hot outside. Why don't you join me to KTV?
W: KTV? Hmm, that sounds fun.

Q: What will Jenny and her friend probably do this weekend?

你會看到

A. They will probably go to KTV.
B. They will probably go hiking.
C. They will probably go out to see planes.

（男）**Jenny**，你這個週末有沒有什麼計畫？

（女）還沒有，我只是在考慮去爬山。

（男）外頭太熱了，何不跟我去 **KTV**？

（女）**KTV**？嗯，那聽起來滿好玩的。

【問】**Jenny** 和她的朋友這個週末可能會做什麼？

【答】A. 他們可能去 KTV。

　　　B. 他們可能去爬山。

　　　C. 他們可能去外面看飛機。

正確答案為（**A**），請在答案紙上塗黑作答。

現在開始聽力測驗第三部分。

Question 21

A. She is very happy.
B. She likes music.
C. She loves the man.

Question 22

A. He thinks the food is nice.
B. He agrees with that idea.
C. He will test it.

Question 23

A. By car.
B. Ride a bike.
C. Call a taxi.

Question 24

A. The terrible story.
B. The noisy play.
C. The loud music.

Question 25

A. She did something wrong.
B. She lost her hat.
C. She is unhappy about the test result.

Question 26

A. Everyone needs to work.
B. Everyone should be on time.
C. Everyone must be like the manager.

A. He travels very often.
B. He has been to Japan.
C. He works for a foreign boss.

A. Because she is cold.
B. Because she is tired.
C. Because she is sick.

A. He thinks Gary likes camping.
B. He thinks Gary is a kid.
C. He thinks Gary is interesting.

A. Their clothes.
B. A piece of furniture.
C. A video tape.

第三組試題　聽力原文及詳解

第1部分 看圖辨義（Pictures）

Question 1

▌試題原文

For Question Number 1, please look at Picture A.
Question Number 1 : What is the relationship between these two people?
　　A. Policeman and robber.
　　B. Customer and cashier
　　C. Bride and groom.

正確答案為（**C**）

▌原文中譯

問：這兩個人是什麼關係？
　　A. 警察和搶匪。
　　B. 客戶和收銀員。
　　C. 新郎和新娘。

▌試題解析

1. 圖片題常會考人物的工作或彼此的關係 relationship。本題很容易看出兩人是新郎和新娘，但是英文習慣上要說新娘和新郎，bride and groom。

試題原文

For Question Number 2, please look at Picture B.
Question Number 2 : What are these two people probably doing?

    A. They are planting flowers.

    B. They are cleaning the street.

    C. They are digging a hole.

正確答案為（**C**）

原文中譯

問：這兩個人可能在做什麼？

    A. 他們在種花。

    B. 他們在清潔馬路。

    C. 他們在挖洞。

試題解析

1. 兩個人拿著工具，卻不像在種花或打掃，答案選（C）。
2. 種花可以說 plant flowers，或是 grow flowers；do the gardening 是指「做園藝、種花草」。

Question 3

試題原文

For Questions Number 3 and 4, please look at Picture C.
Question Number 3 : What does the woman do?

    A. She is a dentist.

    B. She is a hairdresser.

    C. She is an engineer.

正確答案為（**B**）

原文中譯

問：這位女士做什麼工作？

    A. 她是一位牙醫。

    B. 她是一位美髮師。

    C. 她是一位工程師。

試題解析

1. 圖中女士在剪髮，當然她是一位美髮師，英文稱為 hairdresser，也
   可以說 hair stylist、hairdoer。

試題原文

**Question Number 4 : Please look at Picture C again.
What is Allen doing?**
　　A. He is cutting his hair.
　　B. He is washing his hair.
　　C. He is having a haircut.

正確答案為（**C**）

原文中譯

問：**Allen** 在做什麼？
　　A. 他自己在剪頭髮。
　　B. 他在洗頭。
　　C. 他在讓人剪頭髮。

試題解析

1. 多數人每隔一段時間都需要剪頭髮，但是英文不能直接說 cut my hair，那是表示自己動手剪，只有很少數人辦得到。正確說法是 have a haircut、get a haircut，或 get one's haircut。答案是（C）。
2. 洗頭可以說 wash one's hair，或 shampoo one's hair。

Question 5

█ 試題原文

For Question Number 5, please look at Picture D.
Question Number 5 : What do we know about this dog?
  A. This dog is kept on a chain.
  B. This dog is sleeping in the street.
  C. This dog house is empty.

正確答案為（**A**）

█ 原文中譯

問：關於這隻狗，我們看到了什麼？
  A. 這隻狗被鏈子鏈著。
  B. 這隻狗在馬路上睡覺。
  C. 狗屋是空的。

█ 試題解析

1. 圖中的狗在狗屋睡覺，不是在馬路上，狗屋也不是空的，只有答
   案（A）的敘述是正確的。This dog is kept on a chain. = This dog
   is chained. 。
2. chain 有「鏈子、連鎖、系列、束縛」等意思。例如：連鎖店 chain
   store，列島 a chain of islands，為工作所困 be chained to one's
   work。

Question 6

Question 6

試題原文

For Question Number 6, please look at Picture E.
Question Number 6 : What do you see in the picture?
  A. The garbage is on the ground.
  B. The trash can is full.
  C. The container is neat.

正確答案為（**B**）

原文中譯

問：你在圖片中看到什麼？
  A. 地上有垃圾。
  B. 垃圾桶是滿的。
  C. 這容器是乾淨的。

試題解析

1. garbage、trash、waste、junk，都是指「垃圾、廢棄物」。圖中的垃圾都在桶子裡，不在地上，答案選（B）。
2. neat 和 clean 都是「乾淨、整潔」的意思。

119

Question 7

For Question Number 7, please look at Picture F.
Question Number 7 : What is the man?
   A. He is a musician.
   B. He is a rock star.
   C. he is a pilot.

正確答案為（**A**）

問：這位男士做什麼工作？
   A. 他是一位音樂家。
   B. 他是一位搖滾明星。
   C. 他是一位飛行員。

1. 從事音樂的作詞、作曲、演奏，都可稱為 musician「音樂人、音樂家」。男士在拉小提琴 violin，答案選（A）。-ian 結尾的字，和 -ien，-ist，-er，-or 一樣都是指「人」。
2. pilot 是飛行員，或是港口的領航員。

Question 8

試題原文

For Questions Number 8 and 9, please look at Picture G.
Question Number 8 : Where is the car?

    A. It's in the parking lot.

    B. It's in front of the police station.

    C. It's next to a sign.

正確答案為（**C**）

原文中譯

問：這輛車子在什麼地方？

    A. 它在停車場。

    B. 它在警察局前面。

    C. 它在標誌旁邊。

試題解析

1. 這一題考相關位置，in front of 是「在……的前面」，next to 是「在……的旁邊」。
2. sign 指「標誌、告示牌、招牌、徵兆、信號」等。

Question 9

█ 試題原文

Question Number 9 : Please look at Picture G again.
What will the policeman probably do next?
　　A. Write a parking ticket.
　　B. Pull the car over.
　　C. Drive the car.

正確答案為（**A**）

█ 原文中譯

問：警察先生接下來可能做什麼事情？
　　A. 開停車罰單。
　　B. 把車子開到路邊。
　　C. 開車。

█ 試題解析

1. 交通罰單也稱為 ticket，a parking ticket 是「違規停車罰單」，a speeding ticket 是「超速罰單」。警察看到車輛違規停放，應該會開罰單，所以答案選（A）
2. pull over 是把車開到路邊停下來，完整地說是："Pull the car over to the side of the road."。

■ 試題原文

For Question Number 10, please look at Picture H.
Question Number 10 : What is true about these watches?
    A. Both watches are under 5000 dollars.
    B. It will cost more than ten thousand dollars for two.
    C. The man's watch is less expensive.

正確答案為（**B**）

■ 原文中譯

問：關於這些手錶，何者敘述正確？
    A. 兩支手錶都在 5000 元以下。
    B. 兩支手錶要價超過一萬元。
    C. 男錶比較便宜。

■ 試題解析

1. 圖中只有女錶低於 5000 元，答案（A）不正確，而且男錶價格較高，答案（C）也不對，因此選（B）。
2. 比較的時候，用 more 是加強的意思，用 less 是減弱的意思。例如：more convenient 是「比較方便」，例如：less convenient 是「比較不方便」。

第2部分 問答（Question & Response）

Question 11

試題原文

May I see your passport, please?
    A. Yes. Here you are.
    B. No problem.
    C. No, I'm sorry.

正確答案為（**A**）

原文中譯

問：請讓我看一下你的護照。
    A. 好的，在這裡。
    B. 沒問題。
    C. 很抱歉，不可以。

試題解析

1. 把對方索取或要看的東西遞給他，英文最恰當的說法就是："Here you are."。還有 "Here you go."、"Here it is."（用於單數）、"Here they are."（用於複數），都是一樣的意思。
2. 答案（C）"No, I'm sorry." 表示拒絕的意思，但在檢查證件時不得拒絕。

■ 試題原文

How do you want to send this package?
A. Wrap it up, please.
B. Airmail, please.
C. By bus.

正確答案為（**B**）

■ 原文中譯

問：你的包裹要怎麼寄？
A. 請把它包裝起來。
B. 寄航空的。
C. 坐公車。

■ 試題解析

1. 寄航空 by airmail 是郵寄包裹的方式之一，（B）是正確答案。
2. "Wrap it up, please." 尤其是在買了禮物之後，請店員包裝時說的話。wrapper 指「包裝紙」。

Question 13

▌ 試題原文

A chicken sandwich, will this be all?
  A. Yes, medium rare.
  B. And a large coke, please.
  C. It'll be all right.

正確答案為（**B**）

▌ 原文中譯

問：一個雞肉三明治，還需要別的嗎？
  A. 對，五分熟。
  B. 請再給我大杯可樂。
  C. 沒有問題。

▌ 試題解析

1. 雖然提到 chicken，但不是詢問作法，回答（A）並不恰當。
2. "Will this/that be all?" 是店員在確認顧客要購買的東西時所說的話，「就這些嗎？還需要別的嗎？」。顧客如果不再買別的，就說："That's all."；還需要的話，直接說就可以了，所以答案（B）可以對應。

▌試題原文

Will you meet me at the airport?
    A. Nice to meet you.
    B. It's far from here.
    C. Sure, when is your flight?

正確答案為（**C**）

▌原文中譯

問：你會來機場接我嗎？
    A. 很高興認識你。
    B. 離這裡很遠。
    C. 當然啊！你的班機是幾點？

▌試題解析

1. meet somebody at the airport 是到機場接人，所以需要知道班機時間，（C）是正確答案。

Question 15

▌試題原文

What do you want to have for dinner?
   A. I'm very hungry.
   B. This restaurant is very nice.
   C. Beef noodles will be fine.

正確答案為（**C**）

▌原文中譯

問：你晚餐想吃什麼？
   A. 我肚子很餓。
   B. 這家餐廳很不錯。
   C. 牛肉麵好了。

▌試題解析

1. 這一題的重點在問吃什麼，必須以食物來回答，（C）才正確。
2. 三餐和甜點所吃的東西，都可以套用以下的句型：have something for breakfast/lunch/dinner/dessert。

I 試題原文

What is your favorite sport?
    A. I like jogging.
    B. There is a tennis court nearby.
    C. I need to buy running shoes.

正確答案為（**A**）

I 原文中譯

問：你最喜歡什麼運動？
    A. 我喜歡慢跑。
    B. 附近有一個網球場。
    C. 我需要買跑步鞋。

I 試題解析

1. 三個選項都有提到有關運動的字眼，但是只有（A）的 jogging 是運動項目，是正確的對應。
2. court 是指「球場」，通常是長方形，周圍有畫邊界線，分兩邊對打的球場才稱為 court。例如：網球場 tennis court、籃球場 basketball court、羽毛球場 badminton court。其他像棒球場、足球場的範圍較大，它的場地叫 field；高爾夫球的 18 個洞，像走出一條路線，球場是 course。

Question 17

▌試題原文

There will be a sales meeting next week.
　　A. They are on sale.
　　B. Sorry, I'm late.
　　C. Oh, when is it?

正確答案為（**C**）

▌原文中譯

問：下個禮拜要開業務會議。
　　A. 那些在特賣。
　　B. 對不起，我來晚了。
　　C. 噢！什麼時候？

▌試題解析

1. sales meeting 是指「業務會議」，所以答案（C）問開會時間才正確。
2. on sale 是指商品有特價，或商家辦特惠活動。sales price 是「廉售價、優惠價」。

試題原文

We are going to have a barbecue on Moon Festival.
   A. Let's eat out.
   B. That sounds great!
   C. The moon is very beautiful.

正確答案為（**B**）

原文中譯

問：我們中秋節要烤肉。
   A. 我們出去外面吃。
   B. 太棒了！
   C. 月亮很美。

試題解析

1. 聽到中秋節要烤肉，是好消息，答案（B）"That sounds great!" 表示興奮、贊成，是最適當的回應。

2. barbecue 也可以寫成 Bar-B-Q。

3. festival 指「節日、慶典」，我國農曆的三大節日都可以用這個字：Lantern Festival 是「元宵節」，Dragon Boat Festival 是「端午節」，Moon Festival 是「中秋節」。有時百貨公司或飯店舉辦專題活動，也稱之為 festival，例如：爵士音樂節 Jazz Festival。

Question 19

■ 試題原文

How often do you go to the movies?
    A. I moved here last month.
    B. I have seen it before.
    C. Two or three times a year.

正確答案為（**C**）

■ 原文中譯

問：你多久看一次電影？
    A. 我上個月搬來這裡。
    B. 我以前看過了。
    C. 一年二、三次吧。

■ 試題解析

1. 本題重點在 How often，詢問頻率、次數，所以選擇答案（C）。
2. movie 和 move 的發音接近，要能清楚分辨，才不會選錯。

Where can I get some stamps?
> A. There's a post office on the corner.
> B. You should watch your steps.
> C. It is in the bank.

正確答案為（**A**）

問：我在哪裡可以買到郵票？
> A. 在轉角有一家郵局。
> B. 你走路要小心。
> C. 在銀行裡。

1. get some stamps 是「買郵票」的意思，郵局當然是最佳的答案選擇。
2. stamps 和 steps 的發音接近，容易混淆。watch your steps 是提醒走路要小心，口語和標語都常用到。

第3部分 簡短對話（Short Conversations）

Question 21

▌試題原文

M: I got two tickets for the jazz concert this Saturday night. Would you like to join me?

W: Sure, I'd love to.

M: Really? I wanted to ask you sooner, but I was afraid you would say no.

W: I'm fond of music. I'm always happy to go to concerts.

Q: Why is the woman going to concerts?
　　A. She is very happy.
　　B. She likes music.
　　C. She loves the man.

正確答案為（**B**）

▌原文中譯

男：我拿到兩張這個星期六晚上爵士音樂會的票，你要不要和我一起去？

女：好啊！我很願意去。

男：真的嗎？我本來要早一點問你，可是我怕你說不要去。

女：我喜歡音樂，我一向都很喜歡去聽音樂會。

問：為什麼這位女士要去音樂會？

A. 因為她很快樂。

B. 因為她喜歡音樂。

C. 因為她喜歡這位男士。

■ 試題解析

1. be fond of = like，所以答案是（B）。

2. be happy to do something 表示「樂於去做某事」。

3. 要邀人同行，以下幾種說法都可以： "Would you like to join me?"、 "Care to join me?"、 "Are you coming with me?"、 "Do you want to go with me?"。

Question 22

■ 試題原文

W: Tomorrow is Jenny's birthday. Are you going to give her a present?

M: Yes, but I can't think of anything to buy.

W: She enjoys cooking. Why don't we buy her a cookbook?

M: Great idea, and we sure will have more nice food to taste.

Q: What does the man mean?

    A. He thinks the food is nice.

    B. He agrees with that idea.

    C. He will test it.

正確答案為（**B**）

▌ 原文中譯

女：明天是 **Jenny** 的生日，你要送她禮物嗎？

男：要啊！可是我想不出來要買什麼。

女：她喜歡做菜，要不要送她食譜？

男：好主意！而且我們一定有更多好菜可以吃了。

問：這位男士的話是什麼意思？

    A. 他認為食物很好吃。

    B. 他贊成這個主意。

    C. 他會測試它。

▌ 試題解析

1. 對別人的提議說 "Great idea." 就是贊成、同意的意思，也可以說 "That sounds great!"。答案是（B）。

2. give someone a present 是送人禮物。present = gift，重音要放在第一音節，才是當名詞或形容詞用。如果放在第二音節，則是當動詞用，表示「呈現、提出、頒贈」。

3. think of something 是「想到……」。

4 請注意 taste 和 test 的發音差異。

Question 23

▌ 試題原文

M: I have to call a taxi to take these boxes to the office.

W: Do you need a ride? I'm driving back to the office, too.

M: Oh, you are? That would be great.

W: They look heavy. Do you need a hand?

M: No, thank you. I can manage them.

Q: How will they go back to the office?

    A. By car.

    B. Ride a bike.

    C. Call a taxi.

正確答案為（**A**）

▌原文中譯

男：我得去叫一輛計程車，把這些箱子送回辦公室去。

女：你要不要坐我的車？反正我也要開車回辦公室。

男：噢！你要開車回去啊？那太好了！

女：那些看起來很重，需要我幫忙嗎？

男：謝謝妳，不用了，我自己來就可以了。

問：他們要怎麼回辦公室？

    A. 開車。

    B. 騎腳踏車。

    C. 叫計程車。

▌試題解析

1. 聽到女士問男士："Do you need a ride?"，她還說："I'm driving back to the office"，男士也答應了，可以確定他們會開車回辦公室，而不是搭計程車，所以答案選（A）。

2. 開車的人問："Do you need a ride?"，表示願意載人一程；若想搭別人的車，可以說："Can you give me a ride?"。ride 當動詞，是「騎、乘」的意思，ride a bike/bicycle騎腳踏車，騎馬 ride a horse。

3. "Do you need a hand?" 是問別人需不需要幫忙。give someone a hand 就是幫忙某人。

Question 24

▌ 試題原文

W: Excuse me, can you turn down your CD player?
M: Huh? Oh, I'm sorry. I didn't notice that it is bothering you.
W: The music is playing too loud.
M: I'm terribly sorry. I won't do it again.

Q: What isn't the woman happy about?
   A. The terrible story.
   B. The noisy play.
   C. The loud music.

正確答案為（**A**）

▌ 原文中譯

女：對不起，麻煩你把 **CD** 的聲音關小一點。
男：啥？噢！很抱歉，我沒注意到會吵到你。

女：你的音樂實在放太大聲了。

男：真的很抱歉，我會注意不再這樣了！

問：這位女士對什麼事不高興？

　　A. 恐怖的故事。

　　B. 吵雜的戲劇。

　　C. 大聲的音樂。

試題解析

1. 本題有混淆音和多義字，沒有清楚分辨就會落入陷阱。男士知道吵到別人，趕緊道歉說："I'm terribly sorry."，而不是答案（A）的 terrible story。terrible 是「可怕的」，但 terribly 是「極度地、非常地」。

2. play 是常用字，有多種意思，包括動詞用法：「打球、彈奏樂器、播放音樂、扮演角色」，當名詞則是「戲劇」的意思。對話中提到 CD player 和 playing too loud，都是「播放」的意思，而不是答案（B）的 noisy play。

3. turn down 表示「調低音量、冷氣等」，notice 是「注意到、公告」，bother 是「干擾」。

Question 25

試題原文

M: Do you know what's wrong with Mandy? She looks upset.

W: She failed her math test again.

M: Oh, poor Mandy. She must be very depressed about it.

W: She sure is, and she says she hates math.

Q: What do we know about Mandy?
   A. She did something wrong.
   B. She lost her hat.
   C. She is unhappy about the test result.

正確答案為（**C**）

原文中譯

男：你知道 **Mandy** 是怎麼啦？她看起來很不開心。
女：她的數學考試又當了！
男：噢！可憐的 **Mandy**，她一定很沮喪。
女：那當然囉！她還說她恨透了數學。

問：我們對 **Mandy** 知道些什麼？
   A. 她做錯了事。
   B. 她掉了帽子。
   C. 她對考試的結果很不開心。

試題解析

1. 這一段對話有幾個不好的情緒的用字，如：upset「不高興、生氣」，depressed「沮喪」，和 unhappy「不開心」都有類似的意思。聽到 failed her math test 數學考試不及格，所以答案選（**C**）。
2. hat 和 hate 發音非常接近，是陷阱。

試題原文

M: I saw the new manager yesterday.

W: What do you think of him?

M: He is a nice guy, but he asks all his staff to be on time for work.

W: Isn't it a must for everyone?

Q: What does the woman mean?

    A. Everyone needs to work.

    B. Everyone should be on time.

    C. Everyone must be like the manager.

正確答案為（**B**）

原文中譯

男：我昨天看到新來的經理。

女：你覺得他那個人怎麼樣？

男：他人很好，但是他要求他的員工都要準時上班。

女：不是每一個人都該這樣嗎？

問：這位女士是什麼意思？

    A. 每一個人都需要工作。

    B. 每一個人都應該準時。

    C. 每一個人都應該像經理一樣。

┃ 試題解析

1. 題目是針對女士所說的： "Isn't it a must for everyone?"，a must 指「必定要的事」，就是前面所說的 on time，答案選（B）。

2. 口語常說： "That's a must." 表示「那是一定要的啦！」。a must 也可以指「必定要去的地方」，例如：故宮博物院是國外遊客必到之處，National Palace Museum is a must for any visitor.。

Question 27

┃ 試題原文

W: Where do you work, David?

M: I work in a travel agency. It is a big company.

W: Who is the president of your company?

M: I don't see him very often, but I know he is from Japan.

Q: What do we know about David's job?

    A. He travels very often.

    B. He has been to Japan.

    C. He works for a foreign boss.

正確答案為（C）

┃ 原文中譯

女：David，你在哪裡上班？

男：我在一家旅行社工作，那是一家很大的公司。

女：你們公司的董事長是誰？

男：我不常看到他，但是我知道他是從日本來的。

問：我們對 **David** 的工作知道些什麼？

A. 他經常旅行。

B. 他去過日本。

C. 他幫外國老闆工作。

試題解析

1. 從對話中知道 David 在旅行社 travel agency 上班，但不能確定他經常旅行，也未提到他去過日本，所以答案（A）、（B）都不能選。他的老闆是 from Japan，答案（C）：a foreign boss 是正確描述。

2. 要表達工作的地方，有以下幾種說法：

work in + 地方、區域、公司，如：work in Taipei，work in a bank。

work at + 公司、機構，如：work at a department store。

work for +公司、老闆，如：work for Wunan Publisher，work for Gena。

Question 28

試題原文

M: I didn't see you in the class yesterday.

W: I caught a bad cold.

M: Are you feeling better today?

W: Yes. I took some medicine and had a good rest.

Q: Why was the woman absent yesterday?

A. Because she is cold.

B. Because she is tired.

C. Because she is sick.

正確答案為（**C**）

原文中譯

男：我昨天在課堂上沒看到你。

女：我感冒很嚴重。

男：今天有沒有好一點？

女：有。我吃了些藥，也好好休息了一下。

問：這位女士昨天為什麼缺席？

　　A. 因為她很冷。

　　B. 因為她很累。

　　C. 因為她生病了。

試題解析

1. catch a cold 表示「著涼、感冒」，和答案（C）的 sick 吻合。

2. 吃藥的英文是 take medicine，不能說 eat medicine。生病了要好好
   休息，可以說 have a good rest 或是 take a good rest。祝人趕快好
   起來、恢復健康，就說："Get well soon!"。

■ 試題原文

M: Is Gary going camping with us this weekend?
W: Not that I know of.
M: Why isn't he going?
W: I don't think he is interested.
M: What? You must be kidding!

Q: What does the man think about Gary?
    A. He thinks Gary likes camping.
    B. He thinks Gary is a kid.
    C. He thinks Gary is interesting.

正確答案為（**A**）

■ 原文中譯

男：**Gary** 這個週末要和我們去露營嗎？
女：就我所知，他不去。
男：他為什麼不去？
女：我想他沒興趣吧。
男：什麼？你開什麼玩笑！

問：這位男士對於 **Gary** 有什麼想法？
    A. 他認為 Gary 喜歡露營。
    B. 他認為 Gary 是個小孩子。
    C. 他認為 Gary 很有趣。

▌試題解析

1. 當我們說：〝You must be kidding!〞，一定是對聽到的話表示不相信或不以為然，所以男士的態度是不認為 Gary 會對露營沒興趣，答案應該選（A）。
2. You must be kidding! 也可以說：You must be kidding me! / Are you kidding (me)?
3. kid 當動詞，是「哄騙、逗弄」，當名詞則指「小孩子」。在答案（B）聽到 kid，卻是不同的意思，這就是聽力測驗常有的陷阱。

Question 30

▌試題原文

W: How do you like this one?
M: Hmm, it will be nice in our living room.
W: Yes, it is the right size for us.
M: And I like its color, too.

Q: What are they probably talking about?
　　A. Their clothes.
　　B. A piece of furniture.
　　C. A video tape.

正確答案為（**B**）

女：你覺得這個怎麼樣？
男：嗯，放在我們客廳裡應該不錯。
女：對，大小剛剛好。
男：我也喜歡它的顏色。

問：他們可能在談論什麼？
　　A. 他們的服裝。
　　B. 一件家具。
　　C. 一卷錄影帶。

■ 試題解析

1. 他們所談論的東西是 will be nice in our living room，要放在客廳裡的，也提到它的尺寸和顏色，所以全部吻合的答案只有（B）。

2. furniture 是「家具」的集合名詞，不能加 s。a piece of furniture 是一件家具，複數就在 piece 上做變化。

3. 衣服的尺寸如果不合，就是 wrong size，也許 too big or too small。尺碼的說法是先說 size，再說號碼，例如：10 號是 size 10。

第四章 全民英檢初級聽力測驗題庫第四組試題

第1部分 看圖辨義（Pictures）

本部分共 10 題，請仔細聽每題播出的題目和 A、B、C 三個選項，根據所看到的圖畫選出最相符的答案，並在答案紙上作答。每題只播出一遍，題目及答案選項都不印在測驗本上。

請聽以下範例：

▌你會看到

▌你會聽到

Q. Please look at the picture. What time is it?
　　A. It's twenty-four after ten.
　　B. It's five-fifty.
　　C. It's ten to five.

【問】請看圖片，現在是幾點？

【答】A. 現在是 10 點 24 分。

　　　B. 現在是 5 點 50 分。

　　　C. 現在是 4 點 50 分。

正確答案為（**C**），請在答案紙上塗黑作答。

現在開始聽力測驗第一部分。

Question 1

Picture　A

Question 2 and 3

Picture B

Question 4

Picture C

Picture D

Picture E

Question 8

Picture F

Question 9

Picture G

Picture H

第**2**部分 問答（Question & Response）

本部分共 10 題，請仔細聽每題播出的題目，只播出一遍，再從測驗本上的 A、B、C 三個選項中選出一個最適合的對應，並在答案紙上作答。題目不印在測驗本上。

請聽以下範例：

你會聽到

Hi, Betty, how are you today?

你會看到

A. I'm doing my homework.
B. Pretty good. How about you?
C. It's not far from here.

試題中譯

【問】嗨！**Betty**，你今天好嗎？
【答】A. 我正在做功課。
　　　B. 很好啊！你好嗎？
　　　C. 離這裡不遠。

正確答案為（**B**），請在答案紙上塗黑作答。

現在開始聽力測驗第二部分。

A. I'm fine, thank you.
B. Nice to meet you, too.
C. I'll miss you.

A. No, just black.
B. Yes, I like ice cream.
C. Sugar is sweet.

A. Let's eat out.
B. Your guess is right.
C. Let's go to the gas station.

A. Do you know him?
B. Where did you meet her?
C. Who is your friend?

Question 15

A. OK, where?
B. Coffee, please.
C. This coffee cup is very nice.

Question 16

A. For two years.
B. Three months ago.
C. I live in Taipei city.

Question 17

A. I'm afraid I can't.
B. I don't understand.
C. Sure, what is it?

Question 18

A. Yes, it is.
B. Yes, I can hear.
C. Yes, right over there.

A. At a gift shop.
B. I bought it last week.
C. It's very cheap.

A. I want beef noodles.
B. I want apple pie.
C. I want tomato juice.

第3部分 簡短對話（Short Conversations）

本部分共 10 題，請仔細聽每題播出的一段對話和一個問題，每段對話和問題播出二遍，然後再從測驗本上的 A、B、C 三個選項中選出一個最適合的答案，並在答案紙上作答。對話內容和問題不印在測驗本上。

請聽以下範例：

▌你會聽到

M: Do you have any plans for this weekend, Jenny?
W: Not yet. I'm just thinking about going hiking.
M: It's too hot outside. Why don't you join me to KTV?
W: KTV? Hmm, that sounds fun.

Q: What will Jenny and her friend probably do this weekend?

▌你會看到

A. They will probably go to KTV.
B. They will probably go hiking.
C. They will probably go out to see planes.

（男）**Jenny**，你這個週末有沒有什麼計畫？
（女）還沒有，我只是在考慮去爬山。
（男）外頭太熱了，何不跟我去 **KTV**？
（女）**KTV**？嗯，那聽起來滿好玩的。

【問】**Jenny** 和她的朋友這個週末可能會做什麼？
【答】A. 他們可能去 KTV。
　　　B. 他們可能去爬山。
　　　C. 他們可能去外面看飛機。

正確答案為（**A**），請在答案紙上塗黑作答。

現在開始聽力測驗第三部分。

Question 21

A. The weather.
B. The cold.
C. The clothes.

Question 22

A. A graduation.
B. An interview.
C. A wedding.

Question 23

A. He has run some business.
B. He has visited a friend.
C. He has been on a trip.

Question 24

A. How to draw a picture?
B. Where to put the check?
C. Who is going to the bank?

Question 25

A. He'll pick it up.
B. It'll be sent to him.
C. The police will give it to him.

Question 26

A. This afternoon.
B. Yesterday.
C. Two days ago.

A. He's not hungry.
B. He is late for lunch.
C. The food is not good enough.

A. She is excited.
B. She is surprised.
C. She is worried.

A. He wrote a report.
B. He met a friend.
C. He gave his friend a hand.

A. Grace did.
B. Ms. Chang did.
C. Mr. Black did.

第四組試題　聽力原文及詳解

第1部分 看圖辨義（Pictures）

Question 1

█ 試題原文

For Question Number 1, please look at Picture A.
Question Number 1 : What happened to the boy?
　　A. He is jogging on the street.
　　B. He missed the bus.
　　C. He is waiting for the bus.

正確答案為（**B**）

█ 原文中譯

問：這男孩發生了什麼事？
　　A. 他在路上慢跑。
　　B. 他趕不上公車。
　　C. 他在等公車。

█ 試題解析

1. 看到男孩在跑，但不是運動的慢跑，答案（B）的 missed the bus 錯
　　過公車才是正確描述。He missed the bus. = He didn't catch the bus.

2. miss的意思相當多，有「想念、錯過、遺漏、沒找到、不出席、不見了、失誤、逃過」等等，要從前後文去理解。口語常說的 "You can't miss it."，如果是廣告用語，表示「你千萬不要錯過這個機會！」；如果在問路時說的話，則表示「你一定會看到，一定找得到！」。

Question 2

▌試題原文

For Questions Number 2 and 3, please look at Picture B.
Question Number 2 : What does the woman do?
   A. She is a nurse.
   B. She is a model.
   C. She is a waitress.

正確答案為（**C**）

▌原文中譯

問：這位女士做什麼工作？
   A. 她是一位護士。
   B. 她是一位模特兒。
   C. 她是一位女服務生。

試題解析

1. 旅館、飯店、餐廳等的服務生都是 server，男性是 waiter，女性是 waitress，答案選（C）。
2. nurse 也是「看護」的意思，nursing home 指看護老人的「療養院」。
3. model 除了是大家熟知的「模特兒」，本意是「模型、典範」，例如：a model car 是模型汽車，a model home 是樣品屋，a model school 是教學示範學校。

Question 3

試題原文

Question Number 3 : Please look at Picture B again.
What is the woman doing?
　　A. She is serving the customer.
　　B. She is taking his order.
　　C. She is showing the menu.

正確答案為（**A**）

原文中譯

問：這位女士做什麼？
　　A. 她在為客人送餐點。
　　B. 她在為客人點餐。
　　C. 她在給客人看菜單。

1. "What does the woman do?" 問的是工作性質，"What is the woman doing?" 問的是動作。答案的三個選項都是餐廳服務生要做的事情，其中合乎圖片的正確描述是（A）。
2. serve 和餐飲有關的意思是「供應菜餚、端上食物、接待客人」。serve someone something = serve something to someone。

Question 4

試題原文

For Question Number 4, please look at Picture C.
Question Number 4 : What do you see in the picture?
　　A. A cat is having fun.
　　B. A cat and a doll.
　　C. A boy is playing with a cat.

正確答案為（**A**）

原文中譯

問：你在圖片中看到什麼？
　　A. 一隻貓玩得很高興。
　　B. 一隻貓和一個洋娃娃。
　　C. 一個男孩和一隻貓在玩。

試題解析

1. 貓咪在玩球 ball，不是洋娃娃 doll，也沒看到男孩，所以答案該選（A）。

2. 小貓 little cat 也可以說 kitten，廣受喜愛的 Hello Kitty，kitty 其實就是小貓的意思。小狗是 puppy。

Question 5

試題原文

For Question Number 5, please look at Picture D.
Question Number 5 : Where could the man be?
　　A. In the library.
　　B. In the art museum.
　　C. In the camera shop.

正確答案為（**B**）

原文中譯

問：這位男士可能在什麼地方？
　　A. 在圖書館。
　　B. 在美術館。
　　C. 在照相機商店。

1. 男士在看一幅畫,雖然三個選項的地方都可能有圖畫,但是答案
   (B)的美術館應該是最直接的答案。

2. museum 因展出內容有所不同,art museum 是美術館,history
   museum 是歷史博物館,science museum 是科學博物館。

3. 圖畫統稱 picture,有色彩的繪畫是 painting,無色彩的是
   drawing,攝影的照片是 photograph / photo。

Question 6

For Questions Number 6 and 7, please look at Picture E.
Question Number 6 : What kind of food is this?

    A. Japanese food.

    B. Korean food.

    C. Fast food.

正確答案為(**C**)

問:這些是什麼食物?

    A. 日本料理。

    B. 韓國菜。

    C. 速食。

▍試題解析

1. 這些食物是大家所熟悉的速食 fast food（也是 junk food 垃圾食物吧！）。
2. 另一種「素食」是 vegetarian food。

Question 7

▍試題原文

Question Number 7 : Please look at Picture E again.
How much does it cost in total?
  A. Less than ninety dollars.
  B. Less than a hundred dollars.
  C. More than a hundred dollars.

正確答案為（**C**）

▍原文中譯

問：總共要多少錢？
  A. 不到 90 元。
  B. 不到 100 元。
  C. 超過 100 元。

▍試題解析

1. 這一題簡單心算，應該不難知道一定超過 100 元，答案選（C）。

█ 試題原文

For Question Number 8, please look at Picture F.
Question Number 8 : What is the woman doing?
   A. She is watching television.
   B. She is working on the computer.
   C. She is handwriting a letter.

正確答案為（**B**）

█ 原文中譯

問：這位女士做什麼？
   A. 她在看電視。
   B. 她在打電腦。
   C. 她在寫一封信。

█ 試題解析

1. 圖中的是電腦，不是電視機，當然選答案（B）。兩者都有螢幕 screen。
2. 使用電腦的時候要打字 type，handwriting 則是指「手寫、筆跡」。

Question 9

試題原文

For Question Number 9, please look at Picture G.
Question Number 9 : What is true about their clothes?
   A. Their dress style is different.
   B. Peter is wearing formal clothes.
   C. George is wearing a T-shirt.

正確答案為（**A**）

原文中譯

問：關於他們的衣著，何者敘述正確？
   A. 他們的服裝風格不同。
   B. Peter 穿著正式服裝。
   C. George 穿著 T 恤。

試題解析

1. 在答案（B）和（C）的敘述剛好與圖片相反，選（A）就對了。
2. formal clothes 是正式服裝，casual clothes 是休閒服裝。

For Question Number 10, please look at Picture H.
Question Number 10 : Where do you go to send this package?
- A. To the shopping mall.
- B. To the post office.
- C. To the police station.

正確答案為（**B**）

問：應該到什麼地方寄送包裹？
- A. 到購物商場。
- B. 到郵局。
- C. 到警察局。

1. 這題是考幾個常見地點的說法，必備的用字一定不要弄錯。寄包裹就是要到郵局 post office。不過臺灣的郵局還可以存錢，這是西方國家所沒有的。

第2部分 問答（Question & Response）

Question 11

▌試題原文

Nice to meet you.
 A. I'm fine, thank you.
 B. Nice to meet you, too.
 C. I'll miss you.

正確答案為（**B**）

▌原文中譯

問：很高興認識你。
 A. 我很好，謝謝。
 B. 我也很高興認識你。
 C. 我會想念你。

▌試題解析

1. 第一次與人見面，才會說："Nice to meet you."，也可以說："Good to meet you."、"A pleasure to meet you."。答案（B）是適合的回應。
2. 第二次以後的見面問候語有："How are you?"、"How are you doing?"、"How's it going(with you)?"、"How are things going(with you)?"、"What's up?" 等等，可以用 "Fine, thank you." 來回答。
3. 分手道別時才會說："I'll miss you."。

| 試題原文

Cream and sugar?
    A. No, just black.
    B. Yes, I like ice cream.
    C. Sugar is sweet.

正確答案為（**A**）

| 原文中譯

問：要奶精和糖嗎？
    A. 不用，純咖啡就好。
    B. 對，我喜歡冰淇淋。
    C. 糖是甜的。

| 試題解析

1. 問句雖然沒有完整地說："Do you want cream and sugar?"，但是從上揚的語氣可以了解對方在詢問。有些人就喜歡喝純咖啡 black coffee，什麼都不加，品嚐它的香醇，所以答案（A）是適當的，（B）和（C）都答非所問。

2. sweet 除了形容甜味，還有其他的意思也很常用，例如：It smells sweet. 聞起來很香、sweet music 悅耳的音樂、She's so sweet! 她真是親切／可愛！That's sweet of you! 你真好/你真貼心！

Question 13

▌試題原文

My car is out of gas.
　　A. Let's eat out.
　　B. Your guess is right.
　　C. Let's go to the gas station.

正確答案為（**C**）

▌原文中譯

問：我的車子沒油了！
　　A. 我們出去外面吃。
　　B. 你猜對了！。
　　C. 我們去加油站吧。

▌試題解析

1. out of something 是一個超好用的片語，有「缺乏、從中、在外、脫離、失去、源於、由於」等不同的意思。My car is out of gas. 是表示「我的車子沒油了！」因此答案（C）去加油站 to the gas station，是必然的選擇。

2. 指東西缺乏、沒有了，也可以說 run out。例如：We are out of toilet paper. = We have run out of toilet paper.。我們沒有衛生紙了。／我們的衛生紙用完了。

3. gas 是「氣體、瓦斯」，也是 gasoline 的簡單寫法，指「汽油」，在英國用 petrol。gas 和 guess 發音非常相似，gas 的口形較大。

▌試題原文

Susan is a friend of mine.
　　A. Do you know him?
　　B. Where did you meet her?
　　C. Who is your friend?

正確答案為（**B**）

▌原文中譯

問：**Susan** 是我的朋友。
　　A. 你認識他嗎？
　　B. 你在哪裡認識她的？
　　C. 誰是你的朋友？

▌試題解析

1. a friend of mine = my friend。Susan 是女性，答案（A）用 him 不正確，答案（C）也無對應關係，只有答案（B）最恰當。

Question 15

▌試題原文

Let's have a cup of coffee after class.
    A. OK, where?
    B. Coffee, please.
    C. This coffee cup is very nice.

正確答案為（**A**）

▌原文中譯

問：我們下課後去喝杯咖啡。
    A. 好啊！去哪裡？
    B. 請給我咖啡。
    C. 這個咖啡杯很不錯。

▌試題解析

1. Let's do something. 表示邀約，對方回答 OK 是正確答案。
2. have a cup of coffee = drink a cup of coffee。

█ 試題原文

When did you arrive this city?
    A. For two years.
    B. Three months ago.
    C. I live in Taipei city.

正確答案為（**B**）

█ 原文中譯

問：你什麼時候來到這個城市?
    A. 2 年了。
    B. 3 個月前。
    C. 我住在臺北市。

█ 試題解析

1. 疑問詞是 When，詢問過去的某個時間點，答案（B）的 Three months ago.，時態正確。

2. 一段時間 + ago，要使用過去式；for + 一段時間，要用完成式。如果問句是：How long have you been in this city?，答案就應該是（A）。

Question 17

▌試題原文

Can I ask you a question?
    A. I'm afraid I can't.
    B. I don't understand.
    C. Sure. What is it?

正確答案為（**C**）

▌原文中譯

問：我可以請教你一個問題嗎？
    A. 我恐怕不行。
    B. 我不了解。
    C. 當然可以，什麼事？

▌試題解析

1. 當別人問："Can I ask you a question?"，應該用肯定或否定來回應，只有答案（C）是正確的。
2. 要請教別人問題，除了說："Can I ask you a question?"，還可以說："I have a question for you."。

▊ 試題原文

Is there a post office near here?
  A. Yes, it is.
  B. Yes, I can hear.
  C. Yes, right over there.

正確答案為（**C**）

▊ 原文中譯

問：這附近有郵局嗎？
  A. 是的，它是。
  B. 是的，我聽得到。
  C. 是的，就在那裡。

▊ 試題解析

1. 這一題除了回答 Yes 或 No，還要注意主詞不是 it，不能選答
   案（A）。there 在形式上像主詞，there is 不是「那裡」的意思，而
   是「（在某個空間裡）有……」。
2. 要詢問「這附近有沒有……？」，英文就套用 Is there......near here?，
   也可以說：Is there......nearby?。這是非常實用的句型。
3. here 和 hear 發音完全相同。

Question 19

試題原文

Where did you get this lovely bag?
   A. At a gift shop.
   B. I bought it last week.
   C. It's very cheap.

正確答案為（**A**）

原文中譯

問：你這個可愛的包包在哪裡買的？
   A. 在一家禮品店。
   B. 我上個禮拜買的。
   C. 它很便宜。

試題解析

1. 疑問詞是 Where，回答地點才是正確，答案選（A）。
2. 問句中的get = buy，表示東西在某個地方買的，就說："I bought it at ..."，或 "I got it ..."。

試題原文

What would you like for dessert?
　　A. I want beef noodles.
　　B. I want apple pie.
　　C. I want tomato juice.

正確答案為（**B**）

原文中譯

問：你想吃什麼甜點？
　　A. 我想要牛肉麵。
　　B. 我想要蘋果派。
　　C. 我想要番茄汁。

試題解析

1. 這一題只要知道 dessert 是「甜點」，答案再簡單不過了！dessert 尤指「餐後甜點」，包括蛋糕 cake、水果餡餅 pie、布丁 pudding、冰淇淋 ice cream 等等。

2. 你知道如果 desserts 倒過來寫，會變成什麼嗎？答案是 stressed！stress 有「壓力、緊張、強制、強調」的意思。如果懂得反過來換個角度想，壓力也可以轉化為助力，苦差事也有甘甜之處哦！有意思吧？！

第3部分 簡短對話（Short Conversations）

Question 21

▌ 試題原文

M: Brrr! It's so cold outside here.

W: Yeah, and the wind is blowing. I need to put on a coat.

M: I hope it'll get a little warmer tomorrow.

W: You never know!

Q: What are these two people talking about?
   A. The weather.
   B. The cold.
   C. The clothes.

正確答案為（**A**）

▌ 原文中譯

男：哎喲！這外頭好冷啊！

女：就是啊！又有風。我得去穿件外套。

男：希望明天會暖和些！

女：誰知道呢？

問：這兩個人在談論什麼？
   A. 談天氣。
   B. 談感冒。
   C. 談服裝。

1. 如果你聽到了 cold、wind、warm 等幾個字，絕對不難知道他們就是在談論天氣，答案選（A）。
2. put on 和 wear 都是「穿」的意思，put on 比較強調穿上的動作。
3. Brrr! 是擬聲字，在冷得打哆嗦的時候發出的聲音。
4. You never know! 表示「誰知道呢？天曉得！」，和 Who knows?，God knows! 是一樣的意思。

Question 22

試題原文

W: Congratulations! Robert. I hear you're getting married.

M: Yes. My girlfriend wishes to be a June bride.

W: I understand. It's the best season.

M: We are excited about it, but a lot of things must be done.

Q: What is coming up for Robert?
   A. A graduation.
   B. An interview.
   C. A wedding.

正確答案為（**C**）

原文中譯

女：**Robert**，恭喜你啊！聽說你要結婚了！

男：是啊！我女朋友想當**6**月新娘。

女：我了解，那是最棒的季節！

男：我們都滿興奮的，只是有好多事情要辦。

問 ：**Robert** 即將有什麼事？

　　A. 畢業典禮。

　　B. 面試。

　　C. 婚禮。

試題解析

1. 即將結婚 getting married 就是要辦婚禮 wedding，答案選（C）。
2. 答案（A）的 graduation 發音極為接近 congratulation。Congratulations 這個字一定要加 s，要道賀的事情用 on 連接，例如 Congratulations on your promotion!「恭喜升官！」。
3. things must be done 表示事情一定要辦。即使中文用主動的口氣，英文習慣用被動的口氣表達，例如：這件事我非做不可！英文就說："It must be done!"。

Question 23

試題原文

W: I haven't seen you for a while. Where have you been?

M: I just came back from Shanghai（上海）.

W: Were you there on business?
M: No. I was just visiting.

Q: What has the man done?
    A. He has run some business.
    B. He has visited a friend.
    C. He has been on a trip.

正確答案為（**C**）

原文中譯

女：好久不見！你到哪兒去了？
男：我剛從上海回來。
女：你是去出差嗎？
男：不是，我只是去玩。

問：這位男士做了什麼事？
    A. 他做生意。
    B. 他去拜訪朋友。
    C. 他去旅行。

試題解析

1. 聽到男士說他 just came back from Shanghai，剛從外地回來，所以答案就是（C）。其實 a trip 不限用於旅行，a trip to the zoo 就是去動物園，a trip to the museum 是去一趟博物館。
2. on business 不是為私事，而是「辦公事、洽商」等。如果去玩，應該是 for sightseeing、for a tour，去度假則是 on vacation。
3. Where have you been? 是一段時間沒有見面才會說的招呼用語。

Question 24

█ 試題原文

W: Shall I put this check in your drawer?
M: Don't bother. Just leave it on my desk.
W: Are you sure it is safe there?
M: I'll take it to the bank right away.

Q: What is the woman asking?
　A. How to draw a picture?
　B. Where to put the check?
　C. Who is going to the bank?

正確答案為（**B**）

█ 原文中譯

女：要不要我把支票放在你的抽屜裡？
男：不用，放在我桌上就可以了。
女：放在這上面安全嗎？
男：我馬上就要拿去銀行了。

問：這位女士是詢問什麼事情？
　A. 如何畫圖？
　B. 支票要放在哪裡？
　C. 誰要去銀行？

1. 聽到第一句話：Shall I put this check in your drawer?，就可以確定
   答案應該是（B）。drawer 指「抽屜」，和 draw 畫圖無關，小心陷阱。
2. bother 表示「打擾、干擾、困擾」。Don't bother me! 是叫人「不要
   煩我！」，Don't bother. 表示「不用麻煩了！」，就是 It is not
   necessary to do something. 的意思。
3. right away 表示「立刻、馬上」，類似的字還有：at once、in no
   time、immediately。

Question 25

■ 試題原文

M: How can I receive my order?
W: We will deliver it to your place.
M: How long will it take?
W: Three days or so.

Q: How will the man get his order?
    A. He'll pick it up.
    B. It'll be sent to him.
    C. The police will give it to him.

正確答案為（**B**）

原文中譯

男：怎樣才能拿到我所訂的貨？
女：我們會宅配到你家。
男：大概要多久？
女：三天左右。

問：男士要如何拿到所訂的貨？
　　A. 他要去拿。
　　B. 會送來給他。
　　C. 警察會拿給他。

試題解析

1. 關鍵字是 deliver，表示「配送、遞送」，像送報、送牛奶、買家電送貨到府等都適用這個字，正確答案是（B）。
2. 要問一件事情需要花多久的時間，記得說：" How long will it take?"。其中 take 的意思是「花費」。
3. place 和 police 的發音接近。
4. or so 表示「大約、左右、光景」，放在所要形容的字的後面。

Question 26

試題原文

W: I want to do some shopping this afternoon. Are you coming with me?

M: OK. Where are you going?

W: I'm going to that newly opened shopping mall.

M: Is the one near the City Hall?

W: Yes. It just opened the day before yesterday.

Q: When did the new mall open?

    A. This afternoon.

    B. Yesterday.

    C. Two days ago.

正確答案為（**C**）

█ 原文中譯

女：我今天下午要去買一些東西，要不要陪我一起去？

男：好啊！你要去哪裡？

女：我要去那家新開的購物商場。

男：是不是在市政府附近那一家？

女：對，它前天才剛開幕。

問：那家新開的商場什麼時候開幕？

    A. 今天下午。

    B. 昨天。

    C. 二天前。

█ 試題解析

1. the day before yesterday 指「前天」，就是等於二天前。如果熟悉英文日期的說法，這一題就很簡單，不會被對話中幾個不同的時間搞混。

Chapter 4

2. City Hall 是「市政府、市政廳」。

3. shopping mall 指大型的購物中心，也可以說 shopping center，裡面有各種吃喝遊樂的地方，是愛逛街、購物者的好去處。

Question 27

▌試題原文

W: This roast beef tastes good.

M: It is really nice.

W: Then why don't you try some more?

M: I had a late lunch. I'm still full now.

Q: Why doesn't the man try more beef?
   A. He's not hungry.
   B. He is late for lunch.
   C. The food is not good enough.

正確答案為（**A**）

▌原文中譯

女：這烤牛肉味道不錯。

男：真的滿好吃的。

女：那你怎麼不多吃一點？

男：我很晚才吃中飯，現在肚子還飽飽的。

問：男士為什麼不多吃一點牛肉？

A. 他不餓。

B. 他吃中飯的時候遲到了。

C. 菜色不夠好。

試題解析

1. 最主要的是男士說："I'm still full now."，full 就是 not hungry，答案選（A）。

2. 他也認為烤牛肉味道不錯，但是他 had a late lunch，不是吃中飯的時候遲到，而是吃中飯的時間很晚。這個句子的說法和中文不太一樣吧？！值得學著用看看！

Question 28

試題原文

M: Our new manager, Andrew Lee, is coming today.

W: Andrew Lee? Today? You must be kidding!

M: No. Every one knows it but you.

W: Come on, I just came back from my vacation!

Q: How does the woman feel about the news?

    A. She is excited.

    B. She is surprised.

    C. She is worried.

正確答案為（**B**）

▌原文中譯

男：新任的經理，**Andrew Lee**，今天要來。
女：**Andrew Lee**？今天？你開玩笑的吧？
男：我沒有開玩笑，除了你以外，大家都知道。
女：拜託，我才剛剛休假回來呢！

問：女士對這個消息感覺如何？
    A. 她很興奮。
    B. 她很訝異。
    C. 她很擔心。

▌試題解析

1. 這一題是考語氣 tone。從她連續反問，還說："You must be kidding!"，可以清楚了解她覺得訝異，答案（B）。
2. Every one knows it but you. 其中的 but 是介系詞的用法，表示「除了……之外」，相當於 except，常用在 every one、no one、nobody、nothing、anything 的後面。

Question 29

▌試題原文

W: Without your help, I could never finish this report on time.
M: What are friends for?
W: I can't thank you enough.
M: Don't mention it. I'm glad I could help.

Q: What has the man done?

    A. He wrote a report.

    B. He met a friend.

    C. He gave his friend a hand.

正確答案為（**C**）

原文中譯

女：要不是有你幫忙，我根本無法準時完成這份報告。

男：要不然朋友是做什麼用的？

女：我真的不知道該怎麼謝你！

男：不用客氣啦！我很高興可以幫得上忙。

問：這位男士做了什麼事？

    A. 他寫了報告。

    B. 他遇到一位朋友。

    C. 他協助他朋友。

試題解析

1. 對話一開始就聽到：Without your help，可以知道男士幫了忙，而答案（C）的 gave his friend a hand 就是 help 的意思。

2. Without your help 可以換寫成 If I had no your help。

3. 從本段對話可以學習到如何表達謝意，如何面對別人致謝，值得記下來善加運用。

Question 30

試題原文

M: Ms. Chang, did you fax the application form to Mr. Black?

W: No. I've been busy, but I asked Grace to do it for me.

M: And did he get the fax?

W: I'll go check with him later.

Q: Who faxed the application form?
   A. Grace did.
   B. Ms. Chang did.
   C. Mr. Black did.

正確答案為（**A**）

原文中譯

男：張小姐，你把申請表傳真給 **Black** 先生了嗎？

女：沒有，我一直很忙，不過我請 **Grace** 幫我傳。

男：那對方收到了嗎？

女：我等一下會跟他確認。

問：誰傳真了申請表？
   A. Grace。
   B. 張小姐。
   C. Black 先生。

1. 張小姐說：＂I asked Grace to do it for me.＂，因此答案是（A）。選項中的人在對話中都有提到，要特別注意問題的重點，才不會張冠李戴。

2. apply 是「申請」的動詞，application 是名詞，application form 是「申請表」。

第五章 全民英檢初級聽力測驗題庫第五組試題

第1部分 看圖辨義（Pictures）

本部分共 10 題，請仔細聽每題播出的題目和 A、B、C 三個選項，
根據所看到的圖畫選出最相符的答案，並在答案紙上作答。每題只播
出一遍，題目及答案選項都不印在測驗本上。

請聽以下範例：

▌ 你會看到

▌ 你會聽到

Q. Please look at the picture. What time is it?

A. It's twenty-four after ten.

B. It's five-fifty.

C. It's ten to five.

【問】請看圖片，現在是幾點？

【答】A. 現在是 10 點 24 分。

　　　B. 現在是 5 點 50 分。

　　　C. 現在是 4 點 50 分。

正確答案為（**C**），請在答案紙上塗黑作答。

現在開始聽力測驗第一部分。

Question 1

Picture A

Question 2

Picture B

Question 3 and 4

Picture C

Picture D

Picture E

Question 7

Picture F

Question 8

Picture G

Picture H

第**2**部分 問答（Question & Response）

本部分共 10 題，請仔細聽每題播出的題目，只播出一遍，再從測驗本上的 A、B、C 三個選項中選出一個最適合的對應，並在答案紙上作答。題目不印在測驗本上。

請聽以下範例：

你會聽到

Hi, Betty, how are you today?

你會看到

A. I'm doing my homework.
B. Pretty good. How about you?
C. It's not far from here.

試題中譯

【問】嗨！**Betty**，你今天好嗎？
【答】A. 我正在做功課。
　　　B. 很好啊！你好嗎？
　　　C. 離這裡不遠。

正確答案為（**B**），請在答案紙上塗黑作答。

現在開始聽力測驗第二部分。

Question 11

A. She's from Canada.
B. She came from South Africa.
C. It is from New York to Miami.

Question 12

A. Yes, I have been there.
B. Yes, it is very nice.
C. Yes, they are very friendly.

Question 13

A. It was very scary.
B. About once a month.
C. I just moved in.

Question 14

A. I don't think so.
B. It sounds interesting.
C. He is a nice people.

Question 15

A. What are you looking for?
B. We had a good time.
C. So am I.

Question 16

A. Of course.
B. You can try again.
C. No, it's not on.

Question 17

A. Wait a moment.
B. What's on your mind?
C. Not at all.

Question 18

A. I'm glad you like them.
B. It is very nice.
C. They are very quick.

A. My brother was.
B. It was my cousin.
C. I'm walking to school.

A. No, I can't.
B. Yes, I eat a lot.
C. Yes, very much.

第3部分 簡短對話（Short Conversations）

本部分共 10 題，請仔細聽每題播出的一段對話和一個問題，每段對話和問題播出二遍，然後再從測驗本上的 A、B、C 三個選項中選出一個最適合的答案，並在答案紙上作答。對話內容和問題不印在測驗本上。

請聽以下範例：

你會聽到

M: Do you have any plans for this weekend, Jenny?
W: Not yet. I'm just thinking about going hiking.
M: It's too hot outside. Why don't you join me to KTV?
W: KTV? Hmm, that sounds fun.

Q: What will Jenny and her friend probably do this weekend?

你會看到

A. They will probably go to KTV.
B. They will probably go hiking.
C. They will probably go out to see planes.

（男）**Jenny**，你這個週末有沒有什麼計畫？
（女）還沒有，我只是在考慮去爬山。
（男）外頭太熱了，何不跟我去 **KTV**？
（女）**KTV**？嗯，那聽起來滿好玩的。

【問】**Jenny** 和她的朋友這個週末可能會做什麼？
【答】A. 他們可能去 KTV。
　　　B. 他們可能去爬山。
　　　C. 他們可能去外面看飛機。

正確答案為（**A**），請在答案紙上塗黑作答。

現在開始聽力測驗第三部分。

Question 21

A. A trip.
B. A business deal.
C. The sun and the moon.

Question 22

A. He worked late.
B. His father is sick.
C. He is very serious.

Question 23

A. She likes pizza.
B. She doesn't want to cook.
C. She is very hungry.

Question 24

A. He's a taxi driver.
B. He sells tickets.
C. He is a police officer.

Question 25

A. By the seashore.
B. In the museum.
C. On the train.

Question 26

A. They are teacher and student.
B. They are designer and customer.
C. They are schoolmates.

A. He's looking for a job.
B. He's going to work next week.
C. He's a lucky man.

A. She will lend him money.
B. She will pay for it.
C. She likes ice cream.

A. Next morning.
B. In the afternoon.
C. Anytime today.

A. He's asking for directions.
B. He's helping the woman.
C. He's doing something wrong.

第五組試題 聽力原文及詳解

第1部分 看圖辨義（Pictures）

Question 1

▌試題原文

For Question Number 1, please look at Picture A.
Question Number 1：What is this?
　　A. It is a fire engine.
　　B. It is an ambulance.
　　C. It is a taxicab.

正確答案為（**B**）

▌原文中譯

問：這是什麼？
　　A. 這是一輛救火車。
　　B. 這是一輛救護車。
　　C. 這是一輛計程車。

▌試題解析

1. 這是考對車輛名稱的了解。救護車是 ambulance，答案選（B）。救
護車最好不需要坐，但是緊急時一定要懂得如何說：「叫救護
車！」，Call an ambulance！

2. 救火車是 fire engine，消防隊員是 fireman/fire fighter，消防隊是 fire station。

3. taxi，cab，taxicab 都是指計程車。

Question 2

試題原文

For Question Number 2, please look at Picture B.
Question Number 2 : What is the man doing?
    A. He is driving.
    B. He is skating.
    C. He is skiing.

正確答案為（**C**）

原文中譯

問：這位男士在做什麼？
    A. 他在開車。
    B. 他在溜冰。
    C. 他在滑雪。

試題解析

1. skating 是溜冰，skiing 是滑雪，不要混淆。圖中的人在滑雪，答案是（C）。skis 是滑雪板、雪屐，skiing suit 是滑雪裝，另外在水上的滑水 water skiing 也是很刺激的運動。

2. skates 是溜冰鞋，ice-skating 強調在冰上的溜冰，roller-skating 則是輪式的溜冰，室內溜冰場稱為 rink。年輕朋友喜歡玩的滑板是skateboard。

Question 3

┃ 試題原文

For Questions Number 3 and 4, please look at Picture C.
Question Number 3 : What do you see in the picture?
　　A. One is wearing glasses.
　　B. They are looking at some papers.
　　C. They are very sad.

正確答案為（**A**）

┃ 原文中譯

問：你在圖片中看到什麼？
　　A. 有一位戴著眼鏡。
　　B. 他們在看一些報告。
　　C. 他們很難過。

┃ 試題解析

1. 圖中的人有一位戴著眼鏡，拿的是書，神情並沒有顯得難過，只有答案（A）是正確描述。

試題原文

Question Number 4 : Please look at Picture C again.
What do you think they are doing?

    A. They are playing computer games.

    B. They are studying together.

    C. They are riding bikes.

正確答案為（**B**）

原文中譯

問：你認為他們在做什麼？

    A. 他們在玩電腦遊戲。

    B. 他們一起在唸書。

    C. 他們在騎腳踏車。

試題解析

1. 圖片考題，沒看到的東西就不必考慮。圖中沒有看到電腦，不是（A）；他們在看書，該選答案（B）。也許因為 reading books 和 riding bikes 聽起來有些相近，會誤以為是（C）才對。

Question 5

試題原文

For Question Number 5, please look at Picture D.
Question Number 5 : Who are these two people?
   A. Cook and waitress
   B. Boss and secretary.
   C. Dentist and patient.

正確答案為（**B**）

原文中譯

問：這兩位是什麼人？
   A. 廚師和女服務生。
   B. 老闆和祕書。
   C. 牙醫和病患。

試題解析

1. 圖片中有辦公桌，而非餐桌或醫療椅，讓我們清楚辨識這是辦公情境 office setting，答案選（B）。

試題原文

For Question Number 6, please look at Picture E.
Question Number 6 : What is true about this picture?

　　A. The door is not open.

　　B. No one is taking the elevator.

　　C. The escalator is going up.

正確答案為（**B**）

原文中譯

問：關於圖片，何者正確？

　　A. 門沒有打開。

　　B. 沒有人在搭乘電梯。

　　C. 這電扶梯是往上的。

試題解析

1. 如果能清楚分辨 elevator 和 escalator，這一題就很簡單。elevator
　　是上下升降的電梯，辦公大樓多用此。escalator 是階梯式的電扶
　　梯，在捷運站、百貨公司常見。

Question 7

▌試題原文

For Question Number 7, please look at Picture F.
Question Number 7 : What is the girl doing?
   A. She is washing the dishes.
   B. She is taking a shower.
   C. She is cleaning her face.

正確答案為（**C**）

▌原文中譯

問：這女孩在做什麼？
   A. 她在洗碗筷。
   B. 她在沖澡。
   C. 她在洗臉。

▌試題解析

1. 這一題考日常生活用語，三個選項都是需要用水的動作，但合乎圖片
   的是答案（**C**）。
2. 英文講到身體部位 parts of body 時，一定要加上人稱所有格，這是
   中文沒有的。例如：我洗臉 I wash my face、他刷牙 He brushes his
   teeth、去洗手 Go wash your hands。

試題原文

For Question Number 8, please look at Picture G.
Question Number 8 : Where are the house and the trees?

    A. They are in the countryside.

    B. They are in a big city.

    C. They are on a busy street.

正確答案為（**A**）

原文中譯

問：這些房子和樹在什麼地方？

    A. 他們在鄉間。

    B. 他們在大都市。

    C. 他們在繁忙的街道上。

試題解析

1. 圖中的景象可以清楚辨識，不在都市而是鄉間，答案是（A）。
2. in the country 可能是「在這個國家」或「在鄉下」，countryside 指「鄉間」。

Question 9

試題原文

For Questions Number 9 and 10, please look at Picture H.
Question Number 9 : What is happening in this store?
　　A. Some people are waiting in line.
　　B. The store opens 24 hours a day.
　　C. People are changing money.

正確答案為（**A**）

原文中譯

問：店裡現在是什麼情形？
　　A. 有些人在排隊。
　　B. 商店 24 小時營業。
　　C. 有人在換錢。

試題解析

1. 圖中的人是在排隊付錢，不是換錢，答案是（A）。
2. wait in line，stand in line，get in line，都是指「排隊」。懂得排隊、願意排隊，是文明教化的體現，因為排隊表示尊重「先來後到」的原則，First come, first served.。

試題原文

Question Number 10 : Please look at Picture H again.
Who is the man at the counter?

    A. He is a salesperson.

    B. He is a bank manager.

    C. He is a cashier.

正確答案為（**C**）

原文中譯

問：在櫃檯裡的是什麼人？

    A. 他是一個業務員。

    B. 他是一個銀行經理。

    C. 他是一個收銀員。

試題解析

1. salesperson 指出外向客戶拉生意的「業務員」，和店員不一樣。店內售貨員是 sales clerk，出納或結帳人員是 cashier，所以本題答案是（**C**）。

第2部分 問答（Question & Response）

Question 11

▌試題原文

Where does Julie come from?
　　A. She's from Canada.
　　B. She came from South Africa.
　　C. It is from New York to Miami.

正確答案為（**A**）

▌原文中譯

問：**Julie** 是哪裡人？
　　A. 她是加拿大人。
　　B. 她從南非過來。
　　C. 那是從紐約到邁阿密。

▌試題解析

1. 要告訴別人你是哪裡人，可以說："I'm from ..."、"I come from ..."，但是千萬別說："I'm come from ..."，這是常聽到的錯誤。
2. 答案（**A**）是正確回應，答案（**B**）用過去式不對應，答案（**C**）雖然用了 from，卻是表示距離或範圍的說法。

▌試題原文

Have you ever tried Hakka food?
　　A. Yes, I have been there.
　　B. Yes, it is very nice.
　　C. Yes, they are very friendly.

正確答案為（**B**）

▌原文中譯

問：你吃過客家菜嗎？
　　A. 有，我去過那裏。
　　B. 有，很好吃。
　　C. 有，他們很友善。

▌試題解析

1. 這一題的重點在主詞的對應，food 應該用 it 來表示，答案選（B）。
2. 食物好吃可以說：It is nice. / It tastes good. / It is tasty. / It is delicious. 小朋友還喜歡說：It is yummy.。不過 It is delicious. 較適合用在高級料理、昂貴食品。

Question 13

試題原文

How did you like this movie?
　　A. It was very scary.
　　B. About once a month.
　　C. I just moved in.

正確答案為（**A**）

原文中譯

問：你覺得這部電影怎麼樣？
　　A. 滿恐怖的。
　　B. 大概一個月一次。
　　C. 我才剛搬進來。

試題解析

1. How do you like something? 是問感覺或看法，（A）是對應的答案。答案（B）該是回應 How often 的答案。

2. scare 表示「害怕、驚嚇」，覺得害怕是 feel scared，scary 是形容事物恐怖的、嚇人的，a scary movie 是驚悚的電影。

█ 試題原文

What do you think of his suggestion?
    A. I don't think so.
    B. It sounds interesting.
    C. He is a nice people.

正確答案為（**B**）

█ 原文中譯

問：你覺得他的建議如何？
    A. 我認為不是這樣。
    B. 聽起來滿有意思的。
    C. 他是好人。

█ 試題解析

1. What do you think of someone/something? 是詢問對某人或某件事的看法。題目問的是 his suggestion，談事情而非談人，答案該選（B）。

Question 15

▌ 試題原文

I'm looking forward to the vacation.
> A. What are you looking for?
> B. We had a good time.
> C. So am I.

正確答案為（**C**）

▌ 原文中譯

問：我很期待假期快來。
> A. 你在找什麼？
> B. 我們玩得很愉快。
> C. 我也是。

▌ 試題解析

1. look forward to something 表示「很期待、盼望到來」，而 look for something 表示「尋找」，所以（A）不是答案。

2. 對應的句子時間要一致，答案（B）用過去式的 had a good time，無法回答未來式的 looking forward to。雖然語意上，「期待假期」和「玩得愉快」看似對應，（B）並不是正確答案。

3. So am I. 把 So 放在前面是強調「這正是」我的想法或情形，等於 I am, too.，所以選答案（C）。這個用法要特別注意所用的 Be 動詞或助動詞要和對應句吻合。

Question 16

▌ 試題原文

Can I try it on?
   A. Of course.
   B. You can try again.
   C. No, it's not on.

正確答案為（**A**）

▌ 原文中譯

問：我可以試穿嗎？
   A. 當然可以。
   B. 你可以再試試看。
   C. 不，沒有開著。

▌ 試題解析

1. Can I try it/these on? 是購買衣物要試穿、試戴時，詢問店員的話。
   肯定的回答包括：Of course、Sure、Certainly、No problem。答案
   （A）正確。
2. 用字相同，意思不同，是聽力測驗中常有的陷阱，本題的（B）和
   （C）都是如此。

Question 17

▌試題原文

Would you mind waiting here?
　　A. Wait a moment.
　　B. What's on your mind?
　　C. Not at all.

正確答案為（**C**）

▌原文中譯

問：你介意在這裡等嗎？
　　A. 等一下。
　　B. 你心裡在想什麼？
　　C. 沒有問題。

▌試題解析

1. 本題是指標性的考題，重點有兩個。重點一，mind 的後面要加 Ving 或 if 子句。Would you mind + Ving 是請對方做一件事，問他是否願意。例如：Would you mind turning down the radio?，表示「請你把收音機關掉好嗎？」。重點二，否定的回答表示答應，如：No, not at all.；肯定的回答反而是拒絕，因為他介意。這是重要概念，常考哦！

2. mind 當動詞表示「在乎、介意」，當名詞指「心裡」。What's on your mind? 是問心裡有什麼主意、想法。

Question 18

試題原文

These rice crackers taste good.
>   A. I'm glad you like them.
>   B. It is very nice.
>   C. They are very quick.

正確答案為（**A**）

原文中譯

問：這些米果很好吃。
>   A. 我很高興你喜歡吃。
>   B. 那很好吃。
>   C. 他們很快。

試題解析

1. 題目中的 rice crackers 是複數，回應的代名詞一定是 them，而不是 it，所以答案選（A）。
2. crack 和 quick 發音接近。crack 指「裂開、崩裂的聲音」，crackers 指「酥脆的餅乾」。

Question 19

┃ 試題原文

Who were you talking to?
　　A. My brother was.
　　B. It was my cousin.
　　C. I'm walking to school.

正確答案為（**B**）

┃ 原文中譯

問：你剛剛跟誰講話？
　　A. 我弟弟是。
　　B. 那是我表弟。
　　C. 我走路去學校。

┃ 試題解析

1. 題目問的是談話的對象，該是受詞，不是主詞，因此（A）不是正確
　　答案。
2. cousin 可以指八種親屬關係，凡是跟自己在家族中同輩的，不分男女
　　都算，涵蓋「堂兄、弟、姐、妹，表兄、弟、姐、妹」。

試題原文

You like Korean dramas, don't you?
    A. No, I can't.
    B. Yes, I eat a lot.
    C. Yes, very much.

正確答案為（**C**）

原文中譯

問：你喜歡看韓劇，對不對？
    A. 不對，我不會。
    B. 對，我吃很多。
    C. 沒錯，很喜歡。

試題解析

1. 這一題可以回答 Yes, I do. 或 No, I don't.，助動詞如果用 can't，就不是對應的答案。

2. like something very much = like something a lot

第3部分 簡短對話（Short Conversations）

Question 21

試題原文

W: Are you here on business?

M: No, on vacation. I'd like to do some sightseeing.

W: Where have you been?

M: I went to the Sun Moon Lake last weekend. It's beautiful, I like it a lot.

Q: What are these two people talking about?

A. A trip.

B. A business deal.

C. The sun and the moon.

正確答案為（**A**）

原文中譯

女：你是來出差的嗎？

男：不是，我來度假。我要去一些地方觀光。

女：你去過哪些地方？

男：我上週末去了日月潭。那地方很漂亮，我很喜歡。

問：這兩個人在談論什麼事？

　　A. 一次旅程。

　　B. 一筆交易。

　　C. 太陽和月亮。

試題解析

1. 考談論主題的題目，通常都會出現幾個相同性質的字眼。從本題的對談中的一些字，如：on vacation，do some sightseeing，以及 went to the Sun Moon Lake，都指向一個主題，A trip，答案選（A）。

2. 要問外國人來此地做什麼，可以說："What's the purpose of your visit?"。也可以用猜測性的詢問：
   Are you here on business?（來出差嗎？）
   Are you here on vacation?（來度假嗎？）
   Are you here for sightseeing?（來觀光嗎？）

Question 22

試題原文

M: Tony was late for work this morning.
W: What happened to him?
M: He had to take his father to the hospital.
W: Oh, I hope it's nothing serious.

Q: What do we know about Tony?
   A. He worked late.
   B. His father is sick.
   C. He is very serious.

正確答案為（**B**）

原文中譯

男：**Tony** 今天早上上班遲到。

女：他怎麼啦？

男：他送他爸爸去醫院。

女：噢！希望事情不會太嚴重。

問：我們了解到 **Tony** 有什麼事？
   A. 他工作到很晚。
   B. 他爸爸病倒了。
   C. 他很嚴肅。

試題解析

1. 聽到 Tony 必須 take his father to the hospital，所以他父親生病是合理的推論，答案選（B）。

2. 本題最大陷阱在答案（A）。對話中所說的：was late for work，表示「上班遲到」；late 當形容詞用，是「遲到」的意思，work late 表示「工作到很晚」；late 當副詞用，是「晚、到很晚」的意思，如晚睡：go to bed late。

3. serious 可以形容事情、情況「嚴重」，態度「慎重」，人很「嚴肅、認真」。

Question 23

試題原文

(The doorbell is ringing)

M: Who could that be?

W: It could be the delivery boy from the pizza house.

M: You ordered pizza? It's almost dinner time.

W: Yes. I'm too tired to cook tonight.

Q: Why did the woman order pizza?

    A. She likes pizza.

    B. She doesn't want to cook.

    C. She is very hungry.

正確答案為（**B**）

原文中譯

（門鈴響）

男：會是誰呢？

女：可能是送披薩來的。

男：你訂了披薩嗎？都快吃晚飯了！

女：對啊！我今天晚上太累了，不想煮。

問：這位女士為什麼要訂披薩？

    A. 她喜歡吃披薩。

    B. 她不想做飯。

    C. 她很餓。

試題解析

1. too ... to ... 的句型，表達「非常……，所以不……」。從女士所說的話："I'm too tired to cook tonight."，清楚表示她不想做飯，答案就是（B）。

Chapter 5

2. 外送服務是 delivery service，送貨員是 delivery boy 或 delivery man。

Question 24

試題原文

M: Excuse me. May I see your driver's license?
W: Did I do anything wrong?
M: You just ran the red light.
W: Oh, I didn't notice that.
M: I'm sorry. I have to give you a ticket.

Q: What does the man do?
  A. He's a taxi driver.
  B. He sells tickets.
  C. He is a police officer.

正確答案為（**C**）

原文中譯

男：對不起，請讓我看一下你的駕照。
女：我做錯什麼事嗎？
男：你剛剛闖了紅燈。
女：噢！我沒注意到！
男：很抱歉，我要給你開罰單。

問：這位男士是做什麼的？
A. 他是計程車司機。
B. 他是賣票的。
C. 他是警察。

■ 試題解析

1. 男士要求看駕照 driver's license，又說要開罰單 give you a ticket，這些話可以讓我們確定他是位警察。
2. police officer 不分性別，可以是 policeman 或 policewoman。像這樣中性的用字還有 salesperson 業務員、mail carrier 郵差、chair 主席等。
3. 汽車駕駛人可能犯的交通違規事件有：闖紅燈 run the red light、超速 speeding、酒醉駕車 drunken driving、並排停車 double parking 等。

Question 25

■ 試題原文

W: Excuse me, sir. Is this your seat?
M: Yes, here's my ticket.
W: Your seat number is B24, but this is D24.
M: Oh, I'm sorry. I'll go find my seat.

Q: Where is this conversation probably taking place?
A. By the seashore.
B. In the museum.

C. On the train.

正確答案為（**C**）

▌ 原文中譯

女：先生，對不起，這是你的座位嗎？
男：對啊，這是我的票。
女：你的座號是 **B24**，但是這裡是 **D24**。
男：噢！真是抱歉！我去找我的位子。

問：這段對話可能是在哪裡發生的？
　　A. 在海邊。
　　B. 在博物館裡。
　　C. 在火車上。

▌ 試題解析

1. 要知道談話地點，從 ticket 和 seat number，立刻可以判斷這是需要對號入座的地方，答案非（C）莫屬。
2. 當我們問："Is this your seat?"，是為了確認座位；如果要問：「這裡有人坐嗎？」，可以說："Is this seat taken?"。

試題原文

M: Sophia is very trendy. What does she do?
W: She is a fashion designer.
M: No wonder. Do you know her very well?
W: Yes. We went to the same high school.

Q: What is the relationship between Sophia and this woman?
A. They are teacher and student.
B. They are designer and customer.
C. They are schoolmates.

正確答案為（**C**）

原文中譯

男：**Sophia** 很時髦，她是做什麼的？
女：她是時裝設計師。
男：難怪！你跟她很熟嗎？
女：是啊！我們高中讀同一所學校。

問：**Sophia** 和這位女士是什麼關係？
　　A. 他們是師生。
　　B. 他們是設計師和客戶。
　　C. 他們是校友。

▌試題解析

1. 聽到女士說：“We went to the same high school.”，兩人上同一所學校，所以答案是（C）。-mate 是英文的一個字尾，表示「朋友、同伴」，可以構成很多字，例如：同班同學 classmate、隊友 teammate、網友 webmate / netmate、咖啡的朋友——「奶精」 coffeemate。

2. trend 指「趨勢、風潮」，trendy 就是「時髦的、趕流行的」，和 fashionable 一樣的意思。在臺灣常聽到有人說：「她很 fashion」，並不是正確的說法。

3. know someone very well 表示和某人很熟，或是很了解這個人。

Question 27

▌試題原文

M: What are you doing this weekend?

W: I'll probably just stay at home and relax. What about you?

M: I have to prepare for my job interview next Tuesday.

W: Good luck!

M: Thank you! I'll need it.

Q: What do we know about the man?
    A. He's looking for a job.
    B. He's going to work next week.
    C. He's a lucky man.

正確答案為（**A**）

男：你這個週末要做什麼？
女：我可能就待在家裡休息，那你呢？
男：我得要準備下星期二的面試。
女：祝你好運！
男：謝謝！我很需要。

問：我們了解到這位男士有什麼事？
　　A. 他在找工作。
　　B. 他下個星期要上班。
　　C. 他是位幸運兒。

試題解析

1. 只要聽到 prepare for my job interview next Tuesday，就可以了解他要準備面試，顯然這是為了找工作，但還不能確定下週就可以上班，答案只有（A）正確。
2. 祝人好運，英文說："Good luck!"。請注意 luck 的發音，不要唸成 lock，那就變成送人一把好鎖囉！

Question 28

試題原文

M: Hey, look! Ice cream, my favorite dessert.
W: I like it, too. Why don't we go in and have some?
M: I'd love to, but I don't have any cash with me.

W: Don't worry about it. It's on me.

M: Are you sure? O.K. Thank you.

Q: Why does the man thank the woman?

　　A. She will lend him money.

　　B. She will pay for it.

　　C. She likes ice cream.

正確答案為（**B**）

原文中譯

男：嘿！你看！冰淇淋耶！我最愛的甜食。

女：我也很喜歡，我們進去吃一點吧！

男：我很想去吃，可是我身上沒帶錢。

女：沒關係，我請客。

男：真的嗎？好吧，謝謝你囉！

問：男士為什麼要向女士道謝？

　　A. 她會借錢給他。

　　B. 她會付錢。

　　C. 她喜歡冰淇淋。

試題解析

1. 關鍵句是女士說的："It's on me."，表示「我請客，這個帳算我的」，答案是（B）。

2. 請客的說法還有：It's my treat. / I'll treat you. / I'll pay for it. / I'll take care of the bill.（我來處理帳單、我買單）。

試題原文

W: Leo, do you have a minute? I need to talk to you.

M: O.K., but I'm very busy this morning.

W: When is the best time for you?

M: Anytime after lunch will be fine with me.

Q: When are they probably going to talk?

    A. Next morning.

    B. In the afternoon.

    C. Anytime today.

正確答案為（**B**）

原文中譯

女：Leo，你有空嗎？我需要和你談一下。

男：好啊！但是我今天早上很忙。

女：什麼時間你最方便？

男：中飯以後我都可以。

問：他們什麼時候會談話？

    A. 第二天早上。

    B. 下午的時候。

    C. 今天中的任何時間。

試題解析

1. 既然男士說：anytime after lunch，就是指下午的時間，答案選（B）。
2. 要問別人有沒有空，可以運用以下幾句話：
   Do you have a minute?
   Do you have a second?
   When are you available?

Question 30

試題原文

M: Excuse me. Do you know how to get to the National Palace Museum?
W: Sorry, I don't know. I'm a stranger here.
M: Where can I get some help?
W: You can try the information desk.

Q: What is the man doing?
   A. He's asking for directions.
   B. He's helping the woman.
   C. He's doing something wrong.

正確答案為（**A**）

男：請問，您知道故宮博物院怎麼去嗎？

女：對不起，我不知道。我對這裡也不熟。

男：我可以到什麼地方找人問？

女：你可以到詢問台問問看。

問：這位男士在做什麼？

　　A. 他在問路。

　　B. 他在協助女士。

　　C. 他做錯事了。

■ 試題解析

1. 聽到對話一開始說："Do you know how to get to ...?"，就可以知道男士在問路 asking for directions，答案（A）。direction 有「方向、督導、指示、說明」等不同的意思。

2. stranger 不是奇怪的人，而是「陌生人」。I'm a stranger here. 相當於 I don't know this place well. 或 I'm not familiar with this place. 的意思，表示對此地不熟。剛到一個新的環境，或是到外地去，要尋求協助時不妨就說："I'm a stranger here. Can you help?"，應該會有人熱心幫忙哦！

答案總表

		第一組	第二組	第三組	第四組	第五組
第一部分	1	B	A	C	B	B
	2	B	B	C	C	C
	3	A	B	B	A	A
	4	C	B	C	A	B
	5	A	C	A	B	B
	6	B	A	B	C	B
	7	C	C	A	C	C
	8	A	C	C	B	A
	9	B	A	A	A	A
	10	C	B	B	B	C
第二部分	11	B	B	A	B	A
	12	C	A	B	A	B
	13	A	C	B	C	A
	14	A	B	C	B	B
	15	B	B	C	A	C
	16	B	A	A	B	A
	17	C	C	C	C	C
	18	A	A	B	C	A
	19	C	B	C	A	B
	20	B	C	A	B	C
第三部分	21	C	C	B	A	A
	22	A	A	B	C	B
	23	B	B	A	C	B
	24	B	C	A	B	C
	25	C	B	C	B	C
	26	A	C	B	C	C
	27	B	A	C	A	A
	28	A	B	C	B	B
	29	C	B	A	C	B
	30	B	A	B	A	A

Part II 口說部分
Speaking Test

單元一

全民英語能力分級檢定測驗
初級口說能力測驗模擬試題

試題卷

＊ 請在15秒內完成並唸出下列自我介紹的句子：

My seat number is ＿＿（座位號碼）＿＿,
and my test number is ＿＿（准考證號碼）＿＿.

第一部分：複誦

共 5 題。題目不印在試卷上，由耳機播出，每題播出兩次，兩次之
間大約有一至二秒的間隔。聽完兩次後，請馬上複誦一次。

第二部分：朗讀句子與短文

共有五個句子及一篇短文，請先利用 1 分鐘的時間閱讀試卷上的句
子與短文，然後在 1 分鐘之內以正常的速度，清楚正確的朗讀一遍。

One : Could you bring me a glass of ice water?
Two : Please call me as soon as you get home.
Three : Which do you want, bread or cake?
Four : That's the stupidest thing I've ever done.
Five : When will they move to a new place?

Six :
Tina always puts off things until the last minute. She often
postpones her homework until the end of the day. Tina knows her
problem, but it's really not so easy for her to change this bad habit.
One day, she asked for her friends' advice. Her friends told her,
"Why don't you postpone your time for sleeping?" .

第三部分：回答問題

共 7 題。題目不印在試卷上，由耳機播出，每題播出兩次，兩次之間大約有一至二秒的間隔。聽完兩次後，請馬上回答，每題回答時間為 15 秒，請在作答時間內儘量表達。

＊ 請將下列自我介紹的句子再唸一遍：

My seat number is ___（座位號碼）___ ,
and my test number is ___（准考證號碼）___ .

＊ 請在15秒內完成並唸出下列自我介紹的句子：

My seat number is ___（座位號碼）___ ,
and my test number is ___（准考證號碼）___ .

第一部分：複誦

共 5 題。題目不印在試卷上，由耳機播出，每題播出兩次，兩次之間大約有一至二秒的間隔。聽完兩次後，請馬上複誦一次。

第二部分：朗讀句子與短文

共有五個句子及一篇短文，請先利用 1 分鐘的時間閱讀試卷上的句子與短文，然後在 1 分鐘之內以正常的速度，清楚正確的朗讀一遍。

One : What kind of business does he have?
Two : Barney takes a bus to work every day.
Three : You didn't do it, did you?
Four : I go to the movies five times a week.
Five : It's half past nine.

Six :

I often stay up for studying. I know it's not a good habit, but I am used to doing that. In order not to fall asleep, I always drink some black coffee in the late afternoon. My mother asks me not to drink so much coffee or tea because she thinks they are not good things for my body. Actually, I have tried several times, but I think it's impossible to quit my habits.

第三部分：回答問題

> 共 7 題。題目不印在試卷上，由耳機播出，每題播出兩次，兩次之間大約有一至二秒的間隔。聽完兩次後，請馬上回答，每題回答時間為 15 秒，請在作答時間內儘量表達。

* 請將下列自我介紹的句子再唸一遍：

My seat number is ＿＿（座位號碼）＿＿**,**

and my test number is ＿＿（准考證號碼）＿＿**.**

＊ 請在15秒內完成並唸出下列自我介紹的句子：

My seat number is ＿＿（座位號碼）＿＿**,**

and my test number is ＿＿（准考證號碼）＿＿**.**

第一部分：複誦

> 共 5 題。題目不印在試卷上，由耳機播出，每題播出兩次，兩次之間大約有一至二秒的間隔。聽完兩次後，請馬上複誦一次。

第二部分：朗讀句子與短文

> 共有五個句子及一篇短文，請先利用 1 分鐘的時間閱讀試卷上的句子與短文，然後在 1 分鐘之內以正常的速度，清楚正確的朗讀一遍。

One : They are happy when they talk to each other.

Two : He promised that he wouldn't lie to her again.

Three : She told him not to mention the letter again.

Four : He wanted to know if she was still angry with him.

Five : She refused to listen to his excuses.

Six :

My mother is a good mother. She is the person who has influenced me for more than twenty five years. She is a beautiful woman, and she always teaches me lots of things, including some principles of what is good and what is bad.

第三部分：回答問題

共 7 題。題目不印在試卷上，由耳機播出，每題播出兩次，兩次之間大約有一至二秒的間隔。聽完兩次後，請馬上回答，每題回答時間為 15 秒，請在作答時間內儘量表達。

* 請將下列自我介紹的句子再唸一遍：

My seat number is __（座位號碼）__,
and my test number is __（准考證號碼）__.

＊請在15秒內完成並唸出下列自我介紹的句子：

My seat number is ___（座位號碼）___,
and my test number is ___（准考證號碼）___.

第一部分：複誦

> 共 5 題。題目不印在試卷上，由耳機播出，每題播出兩次，兩次之間大約有一至二秒的間隔。聽完兩次後，請馬上複誦一次。

第二部分：朗讀句子與短文

> 共有五個句子及一篇短文，請先利用 1 分鐘的時間閱讀試卷上的句子與短文，然後在 1 分鐘之內以正常的速度，清楚正確的朗讀一遍。

One : I accidentally hurt myself when I was cutting the vegetables.

Two : They usually do their laundry by themselves once a while.

Three : I can't start my car because there is not any gas in the fuel tank.

Four : Bird watching can be done on foot, or even in your own backyard.

Five : A balanced diet and reducing stress can all lead to a healthier heart.

Six :

I came to the U.S. only two weeks ago. However, I miss my family very much because I lived with them for thirty years already. I also miss Taiwanese food, especially for "smelly tofu" . I miss the beautiful weather in Taiwan as well. I hope to like the U.S. after I live here a long time.

第三部分：回答問題

共 7 題。題目不印在試卷上，由耳機播出，每題播出兩次，兩次之間大約有一至二秒的間隔。聽完兩次後，請馬上回答，每題回答時間為 15 秒，請在作答時間內儘量表達。

＊ 請將下列自我介紹的句子再唸一遍：

My seat number is ＿＿（座位號碼）＿＿,
and my test number is ＿＿（准考證號碼）＿＿.

* 請在15秒內完成並唸出下列自我介紹的句子：
My seat number is ＿＿（座位號碼）＿＿,
and my test number is ＿＿（准考證號碼）＿＿.

第一部分：複誦

共 5 題。題目不印在試卷上，由耳機播出，每題播出兩次，兩次之間大約有一至二秒的間隔。聽完兩次後，請馬上複誦一次。

第二部分：朗讀句子與短文

共有五個句子及一篇短文，請先利用 1 分鐘的時間閱讀試卷上的句子與短文，然後在 1 分鐘之內以正常的速度，清楚正確的朗讀一遍。

One : The younger children miss school more often than other children.
Two : We talked to Charles at the party, but neither of us liked him.
Three : I dumped my boyfriend because he only talked about himself.
Four : My husband drove over his bike in the driveway by accident.
Five : All men's haircut are 10% off, even you pay by credit card.

Six :
It is easy to learn how to make spaghetti. First, put some water, salt and oil in a pan. Then, put the pan on the stove for about fifteen minutes. After this, put the spaghetti into the pan for another ten minutes. After that, put tomato juice, oil, salt and meat in, and serve it with cheese finally.

第三部分：回答問題

共 7 題。題目不印在試卷上，由耳機播出，每題播出兩次，兩次之間大約有一至二秒的間隔。聽完兩次後，請馬上回答，每題回答時間為 15 秒，請在作答時間內儘量表達。

＊ 請將下列自我介紹的句子再唸一遍：

My seat number is ＿＿（座位號碼）＿＿，
and my test number is ＿＿（准考證號碼）＿＿．

＊請在15秒內完成並唸出下列自我介紹的句子：

My seat number is ___（座位號碼）___ ,
and my test number is ___（准考證號碼）___ .

第一部分：複誦

共 5 題。題目不印在試卷上，由耳機播出，每題播出兩次，兩次之間大約有一至二秒的間隔。聽完兩次後，請馬上複誦一次。

第二部分：朗讀句子與短文

共有五個句子及一篇短文，請先利用 1 分鐘的時間閱讀試卷上的句子與短文，然後在 1 分鐘之內以正常的速度，清楚正確的朗讀一遍。

One : I am broke. I don't have any money in my bank account.
Two : The teacher always recovers from fatigue by going swimming.
Three : My sister-in-law goes to the health club regularly to lose weight.
Four : Living in the dormitories saves students time and money.
Five : He quit working so that he could focus on his education.

Six :
Do you know something about color tests? A color test can tell you about your personality. You pick up your favorite color, and then a computer will tell you what kind of person you are. For instance, if you like blue, you are a calm and faithful person. If you like red, it means you are a romantic person.

第三部分：回答問題

> 共 7 題。題目不印在試卷上，由耳機播出，每題播出兩次，兩次之間大約有一至二秒的間隔。聽完兩次後，請馬上回答，每題回答時間為 15 秒，請在作答時間內儘量表達。

＊請將下列自我介紹的句子再唸一遍：

My seat number is ＿＿（座位號碼）＿＿**,**
and my test number is ＿＿（准考證號碼）＿＿**.**

* 請在15秒內完成並唸出下列自我介紹的句子：

My seat number is ___（座位號碼）___,
and my test number is ___（准考證號碼）___.

第一部分：複誦

> 共 5 題。題目不印在試卷上，由耳機播出，每題播出兩次，兩次之間大約有一至二秒的間隔。聽完兩次後，請馬上複誦一次。

第二部分：朗讀句子與短文

> 共有五個句子及一篇短文，請先利用 1 分鐘的時間閱讀試卷上的句子與短文，然後在 1 分鐘之內以正常的速度，清楚正確的朗讀一遍。

One : The president has lived in this city since 1996.

Two : Each student has to work hard before taking the entrance exam.

Three : There are many customers in the restaurant as the food is good.

Four : College education of this country has a lot of problems.

Five : News of her son's car accident was a terrible blow.

Six :

I have live alone in Taipei since I graduated from university. I miss my parents very much, yet I don't get many chances to go back home. Last night I heard a knock on the door. I opened the door and saw them standing outside. I was so touched with tears in my eyes.

第三部分：回答問題

共 7 題。題目不印在試卷上，由耳機播出，每題播出兩次，兩次之間大約有一至二秒的間隔。聽完兩次後，請馬上回答，每題回答時間為 15 秒，請在作答時間內儘量表達。

* 請將下列自我介紹的句子再唸一遍：

My seat number is ＿＿（座位號碼）＿＿ ,
and my test number is ＿＿（准考證號碼）＿＿ .

＊請在15秒內完成並唸出下列自我介紹的句子：
My seat number is _＿＿（座位號碼）＿＿,
and my test number is _＿＿（准考證號碼）＿＿.

第一部分：複誦

共 5 題。題目不印在試卷上，由耳機播出，每題播出兩次，兩次之間大約有一至二秒的間隔。聽完兩次後，請馬上複誦一次。

第二部分：朗讀句子與短文

共有五個句子及一篇短文，請先利用 1 分鐘的時間閱讀試卷上的句子與短文，然後在 1 分鐘之內以正常的速度，清楚正確的朗讀一遍。

One : I am to take a math course next semester.
Two : All members of the photography club need digital cameras.
Three : Your dress is really too fancy for the event.
Four : The music was so loud that it hurt my ears.
Five : She traveled for three months in Australia last year.

Six :
When I first came to the U.S., I was very homesick. I married my husband one week before we came here. I left my wonderful family and my successful career. Everyday when my husband went to the university, I stayed in the apartment all by myself. I cleaned the room and washed the clothes. Then, I always thought about my family and friends. What a sad life!

第三部分：回答問題

共 7 題。題目不印在試卷上，由耳機播出，每題播出兩次，兩次之間大約有一至二秒的間隔。聽完兩次後，請馬上回答，每題回答時間為 15 秒，請在作答時間內儘量表達。

＊ 請將下列自我介紹的句子再唸一遍：

My seat number is ＿＿（座位號碼）＿＿ **,**
and my test number is ＿＿（准考證號碼）＿＿ **.**

* 請在15秒內完成並唸出下列自我介紹的句子：
My seat number is ___（座位號碼）___ **,**
and my test number is ___（准考證號碼）___ **.**

第一部分：複誦

共 5 題。題目不印在試卷上，由耳機播出，每題播出兩次，兩次之間大約有一至二秒的間隔。聽完兩次後，請馬上複誦一次。

第二部分：朗讀句子與短文

共有五個句子及一篇短文，請先利用 1 分鐘的時間閱讀試卷上的句子與短文，然後在 1 分鐘之內以正常的速度，清楚正確的朗讀一遍。

One : As a child, I would spend all day with my tutor.
Two : Jenny phoned him when he was watching TV.
Three : She had never seen a book before she went to school.
Four : We pointed out that he had made some mistakes.
Five : I shall communicate with him more frequently in the future.

Six :
I was having trouble adjusting to the weather in Chicago. When I went out for food shopping, my fingers and ears were freezing. Although I tried hard to get used to this kind of cold weather, I still failed to overcome it. In the end, I decided to leave for Los Vegas for a warmer weather.

第三部分：回答問題

> 共 7 題。題目不印在試卷上，由耳機播出，每題播出兩次，兩次之
> 間大約有一至二秒的間隔。聽完兩次後，請馬上回答，每題回答時間
> 為 15 秒，請在作答時間內儘量表達。

＊ 請將下列自我介紹的句子再唸一遍：

My seat number is ＿＿（座位號碼）＿＿，
and my test number is ＿＿（准考證號碼）＿＿．

＊請在15秒內完成並唸出下列自我介紹的句子：

My seat number is ＿＿（座位號碼）＿＿ **,**
and my test number is ＿＿（准考證號碼）＿＿ **.**

第一部分：複誦

共 5 題。題目不印在試卷上，由耳機播出，每題播出兩次，兩次之間大約有一至二秒的間隔。聽完兩次後，請馬上複誦一次。

第二部分：朗讀句子與短文

共有五個句子及一篇短文，請先利用 1 分鐘的時間閱讀試卷上的句子與短文，然後在 1 分鐘之內以正常的速度，清楚正確的朗讀一遍。

One : Flowers are blooming.

Two : The police crack down on a call-girl station.

Three : I read the newspaper for my father.

Four : The doctor pronounced the man died.

Five : She watched me doing the work.

Six :

Studying English takes time and patience, but it is definitely rewarding. People use English everywhere, even for the e-mails. If we can master English, that means we can be more competitive in this international community.

第三部分：回答問題

共 7 題。題目不印在試卷上，由耳機播出，每題播出兩次，兩次之
間大約有一至二秒的間隔。聽完兩次後，請馬上回答，每題回答時間
為 15 秒，請在作答時間內儘量表達。

* 請將下列自我介紹的句子再唸一遍：

My seat number is ___(座位號碼)___,
and my test number is ___(准考證號碼)___.

Notes

單元二

全民英語能力分級檢定測驗
初級口說能力測驗模擬試題

第一、三部分錄音內容

第一部分：複誦

共 5 題。題目不印在試卷上，由耳機播出，每題播出兩次，兩次之間大約有一至二秒的間隔。聽完兩次後，請馬上複誦一次。

1. My father is a physician.
2. What were you doing when I called last night?
3. Turn right at the next corner.
4. It's a nice day, isn't it?
5. The girl who lives upstairs is my friend.

第一部分結束

第二部分：朗讀句子與短文

共有五個句子及一篇短文，請先利用 1 分鐘的時間閱讀試卷上的句子與短文，然後在 1 分鐘之內以正常的速度，清楚正確的朗讀一遍。

第三部分：回答問題

共 7 題。題目不印在試卷上，由耳機播出，每題播出兩次，兩次之間大約有一至二秒的間隔。聽完兩次後，請馬上回答，每題回答時間為 15 秒，請在作答時間內儘量表達。

Q1. What kind of music do you like best? Who is your favorite singer?

Q2. Did you get a present last birthday?

Q3. Have you sent an e-mail lately?

Q4. Do you like dogs? Why or why not?

Q5. What do you look like?

Q6. Do you like summer? Why or why not?

Q7. Your friend is on his way to 7-11. Ask him to buy something for you.

第三部分結束

第一部分：複誦

共 5 題。題目不印在試卷上，由耳機播出，每題播出兩次，兩次之間大約有一至二秒的間隔。聽完兩次後，請馬上複誦一次。

1. Sam always has bananas for breakfast.
2. Is Bob a teacher or a secretary?
3. How does she go to school?
4. I didn't see you two days ago.
5. His family comes from Italy.

第一部分結束

第二部分：朗讀句子與短文

共有五個句子及一篇短文，請先利用 1 分鐘的時間閱讀試卷上的句子與短文，然後在 1 分鐘之內以正常的速度，清楚正確的朗讀一遍。

第三部分：回答問題

共 7 題。題目不印在試卷上，由耳機播出，每題播出兩次，兩次之間大約有一至二秒的間隔。聽完兩次後，請馬上回答，每題回答時間為 15 秒，請在作答時間內儘量表達。

Q1. How do you feel when you see a rat?

Q2. How is the weather today?

Q3. Do you like coffee? Why or why not?

Q4. How long does it take to get from your home to your school or office?

Q5. How far is it from your home to your school or office?

Q6. Why do you want to pass the GEPT exam?

Q7. You need a free ride to the airport. Call your friend and ask him or her to give you a ride.

第三部分結束

第一部分：複誦

共 5 題。題目不印在試卷上，由耳機播出，每題播出兩次，兩次之間大約有一至二秒的間隔。聽完兩次後，請馬上複誦一次。

1. Two and two make four.
2. I'll be more careful next time.
3. We will be meeting twice a week from next month.
4. We would like to exchange this swimsuit.
5. When will you graduate?

第一部分結束

第二部分：朗讀句子與短文

共有五個句子及一篇短文，請先利用 1 分鐘的時間閱讀試卷上的句子與短文，然後在 1 分鐘之內以正常的速度，清楚正確的朗讀一遍。

第三部分：回答問題

共 7 題。題目不印在試卷上，由耳機播出，每題播出兩次，兩次之間大約有一至二秒的間隔。聽完兩次後，請馬上回答，每題回答時間為 15 秒，請在作答時間內儘量表達。

Q1. Where do you usually go for a walk?

Q2. What are you wearing today?

Q3. When is your mother's birthday?

Q4. Have you ever had a blind date?

Q5. Have you ever been on TV?

Q6. What is the best way to get news?

Q7. Your friend is on his way to a drugstore. Ask him to buy something for you.

第三部分結束

第一部分：複誦

共 5 題。題目不印在試卷上，由耳機播出，每題播出兩次，兩次之間大約有一至二秒的間隔。聽完兩次後，請馬上複誦一次。

1. He is building a model airplane.
2. Maybe the show was cancelled.
3. The sign is about movie tickets.
4. Why are you so mean to your parents?
5. Going to movies is my favorite hobby.

第一部分結束

第二部分：朗讀句子與短文

共有五個句子及一篇短文，請先利用 1 分鐘的時間閱讀試卷上的句子與短文，然後在 1 分鐘之內以正常的速度，清楚正確的朗讀一遍。

第三部分：回答問題

共 7 題。題目不印在試卷上，由耳機播出，每題播出兩次，兩次之間大約有一至二秒的間隔。聽完兩次後，請馬上回答，每題回答時間為 15 秒，請在作答時間內儘量表達。

Q1. Besides playing sports, do you do any exercise?

Q2. Did you ever fail a test?

Q3. What's a good kind of book to read during a trip?

Q4. Are you reading now?

Q5. What is something you shouldn't do when you eat?

Q6. Is there a big generation gap between you and your grandparents?

Q7. Your friend is on his way to a post office. Ask him to buy something for you.

第三部分結束

第一部分：複誦

共 5 題。題目不印在試卷上，由耳機播出，每題播出兩次，兩次之間大約有一至二秒的間隔。聽完兩次後，請馬上複誦一次。

1. I enjoyed walking alone in the park in my free time.
2. I have a lot of fun swimming.
3. To become a superstar is my dream.
4. I go to hospital to see my dentist every three month.
5. To grade all these papers by 7:00 will be impossible.

第一部分結束

第二部分：朗讀句子與短文

共有五個句子及一篇短文，請先利用 1 分鐘的時間閱讀試卷上的句子與短文，然後在 1 分鐘之內以正常的速度，清楚正確的朗讀一遍。

第三部分：回答問題

共 7 題。題目不印在試卷上，由耳機播出，每題播出兩次，兩次之間大約有一至二秒的間隔。聽完兩次後，請馬上回答，每題回答時間為 15 秒，請在作答時間內儘量表達。

Q1. Do you shake hands when you meet someone?

Q2. Where's the best place to make friends?

Q3. Who was your favorite teacher?

Q4. Do you think there are too many holidays or not enough?

Q5. What is your lucky color?

Q6. When do you usually have barbecues?

Q7. Your friend is on his way to the library. Ask him to borrow some books for you.

第三部分結束

第一部分：複誦

1. I always go to my school by myself.
2. Please come to me if you have any problems.
3. Your apartment seems bigger than mine.
4. Tommy's grandfather plays golf every day.
5. The hairdresser hurt her hand.

第一部分結束

第二部分：朗讀句子與短文

共有五個句子及一篇短文，請先利用 1 分鐘的時間閱讀試卷上的句子與短文，然後在 1 分鐘之內以正常的速度，清楚正確的朗讀一遍。

第三部分：回答問題

共 7 題。題目不印在試卷上，由耳機播出，每題播出兩次，兩次之間大約有一至二秒的間隔。聽完兩次後，請馬上回答，每題回答時間為 15 秒，請在作答時間內儘量表達。

Q1. What appliances do you have at your home?

Q2. What's your address?

Q3. Please describe your neighborhood.

Q4. Did you work at 7-11 before?

Q5. What kind of food is bad for you?

Q6. How do you lose weight?

Q7. Your friend is on his way to a grocery store. Ask him to buy something for you.

第三部分結束

第一部分:複誦

1. The man has to pay his bill.
2. The girl got her favorite dessert.
3. His mom just ordered a snack.
4. She is buying groceries.
5. The cashier is weighing the mushrooms.

第一部分結束

第二部分:朗讀句子與短文

第三部分:回答問題

Q1. Do you often buy your friends dinner?

Q2. Have you done something romantic before?

Q3. What's your biggest strength in language?

Q4. Are you afraid to see a dentist?

Q5. Do you take vitamins every day?

Q6. What is bad about living in the country?

Q7. Your friend is on his way to a night market. Ask him to buy something for you.

第三部分結束

第一部分:複誦

共 5 題。題目不印在試卷上,由耳機播出,每題播出兩次,兩次之間大約有一至二秒的間隔。聽完兩次後,請馬上複誦一次。

1. One shopper is taking her change.
2. The travelers found their luggage in the lobby.
3. There was much traffic on the highway last weekend.
4. I like living in the city.
5. Amanda needs to make an urgent call.

第一部分結束

第二部分:朗讀句子與短文

共有五個句子及一篇短文,請先利用 1 分鐘的時間閱讀試卷上的句子與短文,然後在 1 分鐘之內以正常的速度,清楚正確的朗讀一遍。

第三部分:回答問題

共 7 題。題目不印在試卷上,由耳機播出,每題播出兩次,兩次之間大約有一至二秒的間隔。聽完兩次後,請馬上回答,每題回答時間為 15 秒,請在作答時間內儘量表達。

Q1. Do you ever buy used goods? What kind?

Q2. What causes traffic accidents?

Q3. Have you ever borrowed money from a loan shark?

Q4. Are you an honest person?

Q5. Do you think taxes are too high?

Q6. Are debates between candidates helpful?

Q7. Your friend is on his way to a stationery store. Ask him to buy something for you.

第三部分結束

第一部分：複誦

共 5 題。題目不印在試卷上，由耳機播出，每題播出兩次，兩次之間大約有一至二秒的間隔。聽完兩次後，請馬上複誦一次。

1. I found the result as I had expected.
2. His friends kept him in the dark.
3. The issue is whether we can gain their support.
4. The movie is on.
5. The music is touching.

第一部分結束

第二部分：朗讀句子與短文

共有五個句子及一篇短文，請先利用 1 分鐘的時間閱讀試卷上的句子與短文，然後在 1 分鐘之內以正常的速度，清楚正確的朗讀一遍。

第三部分：回答問題

共 7 題。題目不印在試卷上，由耳機播出，每題播出兩次，兩次之間大約有一至二秒的間隔。聽完兩次後，請馬上回答，每題回答時間為 15 秒，請在作答時間內儘量表達。

Q1. How often do you go to the museum?

Q2. Do you understand art?

Q3. Do you think we will have enough natural resources in the future?

Q4. Will we all speak the same language in the future?

Q5. Do you like to take a bus? Why or why not?

Q6. Do you buy any souvenirs when you travel overseas?

Q7. Your friend is on his way to a hardware store. Ask him to buy something for you.

第三部分結束

第一部分：複誦

共 5 題。題目不印在試卷上，由耳機播出，每題播出兩次，兩次之間大約有一至二秒的間隔。聽完兩次後，請馬上複誦一次。

1. Experience is a good teacher.
2. The police are investigating the crime.
3. Rice is the staple food of the Chinese people.
4. Neither of the two brothers can speak English.
5. We found the house empty.

第一部分結束

第二部分：朗讀句子與短文

共有五個句子及一篇短文，請先利用 1 分鐘的時間閱讀試卷上的句子與短文，然後在 1 分鐘之內以正常的速度，清楚正確的朗讀一遍。

第三部分：回答問題

共 7 題。題目不印在試卷上，由耳機播出，每題播出兩次，兩次之間大約有一至二秒的間隔。聽完兩次後，請馬上回答，每題回答時間為 15 秒，請在作答時間內儘量表達。

Q1. What was your best vacation?

Q2. What are the best places to visit in Taiwan?

Q3. What is your favorite way to travel?

Q4. Which countries have you visited?

Q5. Did you ever have a bad experience during a vacation?

Q6. Do you like rugby? Why or why not?

Q7. Your friend is on his way to a flower shop. Ask him to buy something for you.

第三部分結束

Notes

單元三

全民英語能力分級檢定測驗
初級口說能力測驗模擬試題

試題翻譯

第一部分：複誦

1. My father is a physician.
   我父親是內科醫生。

2. What were you doing when I called last night?
   當我昨晚打電話給你時，你正在做什麼？

3. Turn right at the next corner.
   在下一個轉角處右轉。

4. It's a nice day, isn't it?
   今天天氣不錯，不是嗎？

5. The girl who lives upstairs is my friend.
   住在樓上的女孩是我的朋友。

第二部分：朗讀句子與短文

One : Could you bring me a glass of ice water?

你可否帶給我一杯冰水？

Two : Please call me as soon as you get home.

當你一到家就請打電話給我。

Three : Which do you want, bread or cake?

你想要哪一個，麵包還是蛋糕？

Four : That's the stupidest thing I've ever done.

那是我曾做過最蠢的事。

Five : When will they move to a new place?

他們何時會搬新家？

Six :

Tina always puts off things until the last minute. She often postpones her homework until the end of the day. Tina knows her problem, but it's really not so easy for her to change this bad habit. One day, she asked for her friends' advice. Her friends told her, "Why don't you postpone your time for sleeping?".

Tina 總是延遲事情直到最後一秒鐘。她常常延遲她的作業直到一天的結束。Tina 知道她的問題，但對她而言改變這壞習慣並不容易。有一天她向朋友尋求忠告。她的朋友告訴她：你為何不延遲你的睡眠時間？

第三部分：回答問題

共 7 題。題目不印在試卷上，由耳機播出，每題播出兩次，兩次之間大約有一至二秒的間隔。聽完兩次後，請馬上回答，每題回答時間為 15 秒，請在作答時間內儘量表達。

Q1. What kind of music do you like best? Who is your favorite singer?
你最喜歡何種音樂？誰是你最愛的歌手？

Q2. Did you get a present last birthday?
去年生日你有收到禮物嗎？

Q3. Have you sent an e-mail lately?
你最近有寄電子郵件嗎？

Q4. Do you like dogs? Why or why not?
你喜歡狗嗎？為何或為何不？

Q5. What do you look like?
你的外觀如何？

Q6. Do you like summer? Why or why not?
你喜歡夏天嗎？為何或為何不？

Q7. Your friend is on his way to 7-11. Ask him to buy something for you.
你的朋友在去 7-11 的途中。請他幫你買些東西。

TEST 2

第一部分：複誦

> 共 5 題。題目不印在試卷上，由耳機播出，每題播出兩次，兩次之
> 間大約有一至二秒的間隔。聽完兩次後，請馬上複誦一次。

1. Sam always has bananas for breakfast.
   Sam 總是早餐吃香蕉。

2. Is Bob a teacher or a secretary?
   Bob 是老師還是祕書？

3. How does she go to school?
   她如何去上學？

4. I didn't see you two days ago.
   我兩天前沒有見到你。

5. His family comes from Italy.
   他的家庭來自義大利。

第二部分：朗讀句子與短文

> 共有五個句子及一篇短文，請先利用 1 分鐘的時間閱讀試卷上的句
> 子與短文，然後在 1 分鐘之內以正常的速度，清楚正確的朗讀一遍。

One : What kind of business does he have?
他是從事什麼樣的職業？

Two : Barney takes a bus to work every day.
Barney 每天搭公車上班。

Three : You didn't do it, did you?
你沒有做吧，你有嗎？

Four : I go to the movies five times a week.
我一週去看電影五回。

Five : It's half past nine.
現在 9 點 30 分。

Six :
I often stay up for studying. I know it's not a good habit, but I am used to doing that. In order not to fall asleep, I always drink some black coffee in the late afternoon. My mother asks me not to drink so much coffee or tea because she thinks they are not good things for my body. Actually, I have tried several times, but I think it's impossible to quit my habits.

我經常熬夜讀書。我知道這不是好習慣，但我習慣如此。為了不要睡著，我總是在下午喝很多的濃咖啡。我的母親要我不要喝這麼多的黑咖啡或茶，因為她認為它們對我的身體不好。事實上，我試了很多次，但我覺得要戒除我的習慣不可能。

第三部分：回答問題

共 7 題。題目不印在試卷上，由耳機播出，每題播出兩次，兩次之間大約有一至二秒的間隔。聽完兩次後，請馬上回答，每題回答時間為 15 秒，請在作答時間內儘量表達。

Q1. How do you feel when you see a rat?
當你見到老鼠時會覺得怎樣？

Q2. How is the weather today?
今天天氣如何？

Q3. Do you like coffee? Why or why not?
你喜歡咖啡嗎？為何或為何不？

Q4. How long does it take to get from your home to your school or office?
從你家到學校或公司要花多少時間？

Q5. How far is it from your home to your school or office?
你家到學校或公司是多遠？

Q6. Why do you want to pass the GEPT exam?
你為何想要通過全民英檢的考試？

Q7. You need a free ride to the airport. Call your friend and ask him or her to give you a ride.
你需要搭便車到機場去。打電話給你的朋友，要他或她載你一程。

第一部分：複誦

共 5 題。題目不印在試卷上，由耳機播出，每題播出兩次，兩次之間大約有一至二秒的間隔。聽完兩次後，請馬上複誦一次。

1. Two and two make four.
   二加二等於四。

2. I'll be more careful next time.
   我下回會更小心。

3. We will be meeting twice a week from next month.
   從下週起我們將一週見面二回。

4. We would like to exchange this swimsuit.
   我們想要更換這件泳衣。

5. When will you graduate?
   你將何時畢業？

第二部分：朗讀句子與短文

共有五個句子及一篇短文，請先利用 1 分鐘的時間閱讀試卷上的句子與短文，然後在 1 分鐘之內以正常的速度，清楚正確的朗讀一遍。

One : They are happy when they talk to each other.
　　　他們彼此交談時很愉快。

Two : He promised that he wouldn't lie to her again.
　　　他保證不再對她說謊。

Three : She told him not to mention the letter again.
　　　　她要他別再提信的事情。

Four : He wanted to know if she was still angry with him.
　　　他想要知道是否她仍對他生氣。

Five : She refused to listen to his excuses.
　　　她婉拒聽他的藉口。

Six :

My mother is a good mother. She is the person who has influenced me for more than twenty five years. She is a beautiful woman, and she always teaches me lots of things, including some principles of what is good and what is bad.

我的母親是一位好母親。她是一位影響我超過 25 年的人。她是一位美麗的女子，她總是教我很多東西，包括一些什麼是好或壞的原則。

共 7 題。題目不印在試卷上，由耳機播出，每題播出兩次，兩次之間大約有一至二秒的間隔。聽完兩次後，請馬上回答，每題回答時間為 15 秒，請在作答時間內儘量表達。

Q1. Where do you usually go for a walk?
你通常去哪裡散步？

Q2. What are you wearing today?
你今天穿什麼？

Q3. When is your mother's birthday?
你母親生日是在何時？

Q4. Have you ever had a blind date?
你有相親過嗎？

Q5. Have you ever been on TV?
你有無上過電視？

Q6. What is the best way to get news?
獲得新聞的最好方式是？

Q7. Your friend is on his way to a drugstore. Ask him to buy something for you.
你的朋友在去藥局的路上。請你的朋友替你買些東西。

TEST 4

第一部分：複誦

> 共 5 題。題目不印在試卷上，由耳機播出，每題播出兩次，兩次之間大約有一至二秒的間隔。聽完兩次後，請馬上複誦一次。

1. He is building a model airplane.
   他正在建造一個飛機模型。

2. Maybe the show was cancelled.
   也許表演已經取消。

3. The sign is about movie tickets.
   這個標誌是有關電影票。

4. Why are you so mean to your parents?
   你為何對你的父母這麼兇？

5. Going to movies is my favorite hobby.
   看電影是我最喜歡的嗜好。

第二部分：朗讀句子與短文

> 共有五個句子及一篇短文，請先利用 1 分鐘的時間閱讀試卷上的句子與短文，然後在 1 分鐘之內以正常的速度，清楚正確的朗讀一遍。

One : I accidentally hurt myself when I was cutting the vegetables.
當我在切菜時不小心傷了我自己。

Two : They usually do their laundry by themselves once a while.
他們通常有時會自己洗衣服。

Three : I can't start my car because there is not any gas in the fuel tank.
我不能發動車子，因為油箱裡沒有油。

Four : Bird watching can be done on foot, or even in your own backyard.
賞鳥可以用行走的，甚至是在你自己的後院裡。

Five : A balanced diet and reducing stress can all lead to a healthier heart.
均衡的飲食與減壓會使你有個更健康的心臟。

Six :
I came to the U.S. only two weeks ago. However, I miss my family very much because I lived with them for thirty years already. I also miss Taiwanese food, especially for "smelly tofu". I miss the beautiful weather in Taiwan as well. I hope to like the U.S. after I live here a long time.

我來到美國才兩個星期。然而，我非常想念我的家人因為我已經與他們同住了 30 年。我也想念臺灣的食物，特別是臭豆腐。我也想念臺灣的好天氣。我希望在住在這兒一段時間後能喜歡美國。

第三部分：回答問題

共 7 題。題目不印在試卷上，由耳機播出，每題播出兩次，兩次之
間大約有一至二秒的間隔。聽完兩次後，請馬上回答，每題回答時間
為 15 秒，請在作答時間內儘量表達。

Q1. Besides playing sports, do you do any exercise?
除了球類，你會做任何其他的運動嗎？

Q2. Did you ever fail a test?
你有無曾經考試失敗呢？

Q3. What's a good kind of book to read during a trip?
在旅行途中的好書是？

Q4. Are you reading now?
你現在正在閱讀嗎？

Q5. What is something you shouldn't do when you eat?
什麼事情是你吃飯時不可以做的？

Q6. Is there a big generation gap between you and your grandparents?
在你與你祖父母之間有無嚴重代溝呢？

Q7. Your friend is on his way to a post office. Ask him to buy
something for you.
你的朋友正在去郵局的路上。請他替你買些東西。

第一部分：複誦

1. I enjoyed walking alone in the park in my free time.
   我喜歡在空閒時在公園內獨自散步。

2. I have a lot of fun swimming.
   我從游泳中獲得很多樂趣。

3. To become a superstar is my dream.
   成為巨星是我的夢想。

4. I go to hospital to see my dentist every three month.
   我每 3 個月去醫院一次看牙醫。

5. To grade all these papers by 7:00 will be impossible.
   在 7 點前完成所有報告的評分是不可能的。

第二部分：朗讀句子與短文

One : The younger children miss school more often than other children.
年輕的小孩比其他的小孩容易沒來上課。

Two : We talked to Charles at the party, but neither of us liked him.
我們在宴會中與 Charles 談話，但是我們沒有人喜歡他。

Three : I dumped my boyfriend because he only talked about himself.
我放棄我的男友，因為他總是在說自己的事情。

Four : My husband drove over his bike in the driveway by accident.
我的丈夫不小心在馬路上輾過他的腳踏車。

Five : All men's haircut are 10% off, even you pay by credit card.
所有男士剪髮均九折，即使是信用卡付款。

Six :
It is easy to learn how to make spaghetti. First, put some water, salt and oil in a pan. Then, put the pan on the stove for about fifteen minutes. After this, put the spaghetti into the pan for another ten minutes. After that, put tomato juice, oil, salt and meat in, and serve it with cheese finally.

學做義大利麵是很容易的。首先，放一些水、鹽巴，和油在鍋子裡。然後把鍋子放在火爐上。之後，放義大利麵在鍋子裡 10 分鐘。然後，再放番茄汁、油、鹽巴與肉進去。最後再加上起司。

第三部分：回答問題

共 7 題。題目不印在試卷上，由耳機播出，每題播出兩次，兩次之間大約有一至二秒的間隔。聽完兩次後，請馬上回答，每題回答時間為 15 秒，請在作答時間內儘量表達。

Q1. Do you shake hands when you meet someone?
當你遇見人時會握手嗎？

Q2. Where's the best place to make friends?
交朋友最佳場所是？

Q3. Who was your favorite teacher?
誰是你最喜歡的老師？

Q4. Do you think there are too many holidays or not enough?
你認為假日太多還是不夠？

Q5. What is your lucky color?
你的幸運顏色是？

Q6. When do you usually have barbecues?
你通常何時烤肉？

Q7. Your friend is on his way to the library. Ask him to borrow some books for you.
你的朋友在去圖書館的途中。要他替你借一些書。

TEST 6

第一部分：複誦

共 5 題。題目不印在試卷上，由耳機播出，每題播出兩次，兩次之間大約有一至二秒的間隔。聽完兩次後，請馬上複誦一次。

1. I always go to my school by myself.
   我總是獨自上學。

2. Please come to me if you have any problems.
   假如你有任何問題來找我。

3. Your apartment seems bigger than mine.
   你的公寓似乎比我的大。

4. Tommy's grandfather plays golf every day.
   Tommy 的祖父每天打高爾夫球。

5. The hairdresser hurt her hand.
   這位髮型設計師剪她的頭髮。

第二部分：朗讀句子與短文

共有五個句子及一篇短文，請先利用 1 分鐘的時間閱讀試卷上的句子與短文，然後在 1 分鐘之內以正常的速度，清楚正確的朗讀一遍。

One : I am broke. I don't have any money in my bank account.

我破產了，我的銀行裡沒有錢了。

Two : The teacher always recovers from fatigue by going swimming.

這老師總是藉由游泳來康復。

Three : My sister-in-law goes to the health club regularly to lose weight.

我的嫂子固定到健身中心減重。

Four : Living in the dormitories saves students time and money.

住宿讓學生省錢與時間。

Five : He quit working so that he could focus on his education.

他辭去工作如此便可專心在學業上。

Six :

Do you know something about color tests? A color test can tell you about your personality. You pick up your favorite color, and then a computer will tell you what kind of person you are. For instance, if you like blue, you are a calm and faithful person. If you like red, it means you are a romantic person.

你知道色彩測驗嗎？色彩測驗可以告知你的個人特質。你選擇一個你最喜歡的顏色，然後電腦將告知你是一個什麼樣的人。舉例而言，假如你喜歡藍色，你是一位冷靜與可靠的人。假如你喜歡紅色，那表示你是一位多情的人。

第三部分：回答問題

共 7 題。題目不印在試卷上，由耳機播出，每題播出兩次，兩次之間大約有一至二秒的間隔。聽完兩次後，請馬上回答，每題回答時間為 15 秒，請在作答時間內儘量表達。

Q1. What appliances do you have at your home?
你的家裡有什麼電器設備？

Q2. What's your address?
你的地址是？

Q3. Please describe your neighborhood.
請描述你的居家鄰近地區。

Q4. Did you work at 7-11 before?
你以前有在 7-11 工作過嗎？

Q5. What kind of food is bad for you?
什麼樣的食物對你有害？

Q6. How do you lose weight?
你如何減重？

Q7. Your friend is on his way to a grocery store. Ask him to buy something for you.
你的朋友在去雜貨店的路上。要他替你買一些東西。

第一部分：複誦

共 5 題。題目不印在試卷上，由耳機播出，每題播出兩次，兩次之間大約有一至二秒的間隔。聽完兩次後，請馬上複誦一次。

1. The man has to pay his bill.
   這個人必須要付他的帳單。

2. The girl got her favorite dessert.
   這個女孩得到她最愛的甜點。

3. His mom just ordered a snack.
   他的母親剛點了一份點心。

4. She is buying groceries.
   她正在買一些雜貨。

5. The cashier is weighing the mushrooms.
   這收銀員正在將蘑菇秤重。

第二部分：朗讀句子與短文

共有五個句子及一篇短文，請先利用 1 分鐘的時間閱讀試卷上的句子與短文，然後在 1 分鐘之內以正常的速度，清楚正確的朗讀一遍。

One : The president has lived in this city since 1996.

這位總裁自 1996 年就住在這個城市。

Two : Each student has to work hard before taking the entrance exam.

每位學生在接受入學考試前必須要努力用功。

Three : There are many customers in the restaurant as the food is good.

這家餐廳有很多顧客因為它食物很好。

Four : College education of this country has a lot of problems.

這國家的大學教育有很多的問題。

Five : News of her son's car accident was a terrible blow.

他兒子車禍的消息是一可怕的打擊。

Six :

I have live alone in Taipei since I graduated from university. I miss my parents very much, yet I don't get many chances to go back home. Last night I heard a knock on the door. I opened the door and saw them standing outside. I was so touched with tears in my eyes.

自從我從大學畢業後就一直住在臺北。我非常想念我的父母,但是我沒有很多機會回家。昨晚我聽見敲門聲。我打開門看見他們站在門外。我感動得眼角充滿了淚水。

共 7 題。題目不印在試卷上，由耳機播出，每題播出兩次，兩次之間大約有一至二秒的間隔。聽完兩次後，請馬上回答，每題回答時間為 15 秒，請在作答時間內儘量表達。

Q1. Do you often buy your friends dinner?
你常請你朋友吃晚餐嗎？

Q2. Have you done something romantic before?
你以前有做過一些羅曼蒂克的事嗎？

Q3. What's your biggest strength in language?
你在語言上的長處是？

Q4. Are you afraid to see a dentist?
你害怕看牙醫嗎？

Q5. Do you take vitamins every day?
你每天吃維他命嗎？

Q6. What is bad about living in the country?
住在鄉下的壞處是？

Q7. Your friend is on his way to a night market. Ask him to buy something for you.
你的朋友正要去夜市。請他幫你買一些東西。

TEST 8

第一部分：複誦

共 5 題。題目不印在試卷上，由耳機播出，每題播出兩次，兩次之
間大約有一至二秒的間隔。聽完兩次後，請馬上複誦一次。

1. One shopper is taking her change.
   一位購物者正在拿零錢。

2. The travelers found their luggage in the lobby.
   旅客在大廳找到他們的行李。

3. There was much traffic on the highway last weekend.
   上週末有許多的車輛在高速公路上。

4. I like living in the city.
   我喜歡住在城市。

5. Amanda needs to make an urgent call.
   Amanda 需要打一通緊急電話。

第二部分：朗讀句子與短文

共有五個句子及一篇短文，請先利用 1 分鐘的時間閱讀試卷上的句
子與短文，然後在 1 分鐘之內以正常的速度，清楚正確的朗讀一遍。

One : I am to take a math course next semester.
　　　我下學期要修數學課。

Two : All members of the photography club need digital cameras.
　　　所有攝影會的成員需要數位照相機。

Three : Your dress is really too fancy for the event.
　　　　你的衣服在這個場合實在太炫了。

Four : The music was so loud that it hurt my ears.
　　　這音樂太大聲以至於傷了我的耳朵。

Five : She traveled for three months in Australia last year.
　　　去年她在澳洲旅遊 3 個月。

Six :
When I first came to the U.S., I was very homesick. I married my
husband one week before we came here. I left my wonderful family
and my successful career. Everyday when my husband went to the
university, I stayed in the apartment all by myself. I cleaned the
room and washed the clothes. Then, I always thought about my
family and friends. What a sad life!

當我第一次到美國的時候,我非常想家。我在到這一週前嫁給我的丈
夫。我離開了我美好的家庭與成功的事業。每天當我丈夫去大學後,我
就獨自待在公寓住所。我清理房間與洗衣服。之後,我總是非常想念我
的家庭與朋友。實在感傷。

第三部分：回答問題

共 7 題。題目不印在試卷上，由耳機播出，每題播出兩次，兩次之間大約有一至二秒的間隔。聽完兩次後，請馬上回答，每題回答時間為 15 秒，請在作答時間內儘量表達。

Q1. Do you ever buy used goods? What kind?
你會買二手貨嗎？什麼種類的？

Q2. What causes traffic accidents?
什麼造成了交通事故？

Q3. Have you ever borrowed money from a loan shark?
你曾經向地下錢莊借錢嗎？

Q4. Are you an honest person?
你是一個誠實的人嗎？

Q5. Do you think taxes are too high?
你認為稅太高了嗎？

Q6. Are debates between candidates helpful?
候選人之間的辯論你覺得有用嗎？

Q7. Your friend is on his way to a stationery store. Ask him to buy something for you.
你的朋友正在去文具店的路上。請他幫你買些東西。

第一部分：複誦

1. I found the result as I had expected.
   我發現結果如我預期。

2. His friends kept him in the dark.
   他的朋友讓他在黑暗中。

3. The issue is whether we can gain their support.
   重點是我們是否可以獲得她們的支持。

4. The movie is on.
   電影在上映。

5. The music is touching.
   這音樂很感人。

第二部分：朗讀句子與短文

One : As a child, I would spend all day with my tutor.
當我是小孩時，我整天都與我的家教在一起。

Two : Jenny phoned him when he was watching TV.
Jenny 在他正在看電視時來電。

Three : She had never seen a book before she went to school.
在她去上學前，她從未見過書。

Four : We pointed out that he had made some mistakes.
我們指出他所犯的一些錯誤。

Five : I shall communicate with him more frequently in the future.
我未來將與他更經常的溝通。

Six :
I was having trouble adjusting to the weather in Chicago. When I went out for food shopping, my fingers and ears were freezing. Although I tried hard to get used to this kind of cold weather, I still failed to overcome it. In the end, I decided to leave for Los Vegas for a warmer weather.

我對於適應芝加哥的天氣有困難。當我外出購買食物時，我的手指與耳朵都凍僵了。雖然，我試著習慣這樣的冷天氣，但我仍然無法克服。最後，我決定前往拉斯維加斯過較溫暖的天氣。

> 共 7 題。題目不印在試卷上，由耳機播出，每題播出兩次，兩次之
> 間大約有一至二秒的間隔。聽完兩次後，請馬上回答，每題回答時間
> 為 15 秒，請在作答時間內儘量表達。

Q1. How often do you go to the museum?
你多常去博物館？

Q2. Do you understand art?
你對藝術了解嗎？

Q3. Do you think we will have enough natural resources in the future?
你認為在未來你有足夠的保險嗎？

Q4. Will we all speak the same language in the future?
在未來我們會說相同的語言嗎？

Q5. Do you like to take a bus? Why or why not?
你喜歡搭公車嗎？為何或為何不？

Q6. Do you buy any souvenirs when you travel overseas?
當你海外旅遊時，你會買紀念品嗎？

Q7. Your friend is on his way to a hardware store. Ask him to buy something for you.
你的朋友正在去五金行的路上。請他替你買一些東西。

TEST 10

第一部分：複誦

1. Experience is a good teacher.
   經驗是好老師。

2. The police are investigating the crime.
   警方正在偵查這犯罪。

3. Rice is the staple food of the Chinese people.
   米食對中國人來說是主要的食物。

4. Neither of the two brothers can speak English.
   這兩位兄弟都不會說英文。

5. We found the house empty.
   我們發現這房子是空的。

第二部分：朗讀句子與短文

One : Flowers are blooming.
花正盛開。

Two : The police crack down on a call-girl station.
警方破獲一處應召站。

Three : I read the newspaper for my father.
我替我父親唸報紙。

Four : The doctor pronounced the man died.
這醫生宣布這人死亡。

Five : She watched me doing the work.
她監視我做工作。

Six :
Studying English takes time and patience, but it is definitely rewarding. People use English everywhere, even for the e-mails. If we can master English, that means we can be more competitive in this international community.

學英文是需要時間與耐性的,但它是絕對值得的。人們在到處都使用英文,甚至是 e-mail。假如我們可以精通英文,那表示我們可以在國際社會裡更有競爭力。

第三部分：回答問題

共 7 題。題目不印在試卷上，由耳機播出，每題播出兩次，兩次之
間大約有一至二秒的間隔。聽完兩次後，請馬上回答，每題回答時間
為 15 秒，請在作答時間內儘量表達。

Q1. What was your best vacation?
你最棒的假期是？

Q2. What are the best places to visit in Taiwan?
在臺灣最棒的旅遊點是？

Q3. What is your favorite way to travel?
你最喜歡的旅遊方式是？

Q4. Which countries have you visited?
你曾經去過哪些國家？

Q5. Did you ever have a bad experience during a vacation?
在旅遊期間有無不好的經驗？

Q6. Do you like rugby? Why or why not?
你喜歡英式橄欖球嗎？為何或為何不？

Q7. Your friend is on his way to a flower shop. Ask him to buy
something for you.
你的朋友正在去花店的途中。請他替你買些東西。

Notes

單元四

全民英語能力分級檢定測驗
初級口說能力測驗模擬試題

試題解析

第一部分：複誦

共 5 題。題目不印在試卷上，由耳機播出，每題播出兩次，兩次之間大約有一至二秒的間隔。聽完兩次後，請馬上複誦一次。

1. My father is a physician.
   得分關鍵：**physician** 是內科醫生的意思，**ph** 發【**f**】的音。

2. What were you doing when I called last night?
   得分關鍵：**What were you doing** 是主要句，**when I called last night** 是時間子句，在朗讀時在 **when** 前可稍停頓。

3. Turn right at the next corner.
   得分關鍵：**Turn** 的 **ur** 要有捲舌音，且稍重音；**next corner** 中的 **t** 會省音，故不用發出。

4. It's a nice day, isn't it?
   得分關鍵：附件問句的部分語調可上升或下降。

5. The girl who lives upstairs is my friend.
   得分關鍵：**who lives upstairs** 在本句中屬形容詞子句；**upstairs** 的 **s** 是【**z**】的有聲子音。

第二部分：朗讀句子與短文

共有五個句子及一篇短文，請先利用 1 分鐘的時間閱讀試卷上的句子與短文，然後在 1 分鐘之內以正常的速度，清楚正確的朗讀一遍。

One : Could you bring me a glass of ice water?
得分關鍵：**could you** 會有連音的效果；本句為 **Yes-No** 問句故語
　　　　調要向上揚。

Two : Please call me as soon as you get home.
得分關鍵：**as soon as** 是一連接詞，表示「當」的意思，唸時要清
　　　　楚。**Please** 中的 **ea** 是長音【i】。

Three : Which do you want, bread or cake?
得分關鍵：這是一個選擇性的問句要先上升後向下降。因此 **bread**
　　　　上升，**cake** 要下降。

Four : That's the stupidest thing I've ever done.
得分關鍵：**stupidest** 的 **est** 發【st】的音。**I've** 的發音要連在一
　　　　起，不可分為 **I have** 的唸法。

Five : When will they move to a new place?
得分關鍵：**place** 的 **a** 發長音【e】的音。

Six :
Tina always puts off things until the last minute. She often postpones her homework until the end of the day. Tina knows her problem, but it's really not so easy for her to change this bad habit. One day, she asked for her friends' advice. Her friends told her, "Why don't you postpone your time for sleeping?" .

得分關鍵：**postpone** 是延遲的意思；**the end of** 是底部的意思。最後一句 **why don't you** 的句型不要向上提升。

第三部分：回答問題

> 共 7 題。題目不印在試卷上，由耳機播出，每題播出兩次，兩次之間大約有一至二秒的間隔。聽完兩次後，請馬上回答，每題回答時間為 15 秒，請在作答時間內儘量表達。

Q1. What kind of music do you like best? Who is your favorite singer?
你最喜歡何種音樂？誰是你最愛的歌手？
參考答案：
I like pop music very much. I like it because some pop music is very touching. I like A-mei's love songs, so A-mei is my favorite singer. I usually go to KTV to practice her songs.
我非常喜歡流行音樂。我喜歡它的原因是有些流行音樂是很感人的。我喜歡阿妹的情歌，所以她是我最愛的歌手。我通常去 KTV 練習她的歌曲。

Q2. Did you get a present last birthday?
去年生日你有收到禮物嗎？
參考答案：
Yes, I did. I got a watch as my birthday present from my mother. I really like it because it is digital and has bright color. I am still wearing it on my wrist right now.
是的。我在生日時從我媽媽那裡得到了一隻手錶。我很喜歡它，因為它是數位的而且有明亮的顏色。我現在仍把它戴在手上。

Q3. Have you send an e-mail lately?

你最近有寄電子郵件嗎？

參考答案：

Yes, I have. I've sent an e-mall message to my classmate. Sometimes I need to discuss homework with my classmate, so I always complete my homework by sending several e-mail.

是的，我是。我有寄電子郵件給我的同學。有時我需要使用電子郵件與我的同學討論作業。所以我都是藉由寄郵件來完成我的作業。

Q4. Do you like dogs? Why or why not?

你喜歡狗嗎？為何或為何不？

參考答案：

I like dogs. I think dogs are the friendliest animals in the world. I have a puppy, and I always play with it. When I feel bad, it is my friend and I can talk with it. I can't imagine the day it leaves me.

我喜歡狗。我認為狗是全世界最友善的動物。我有一隻小狗，我總是和牠玩。當我心情不好時，牠是我的朋友，而我可以和牠說話。我無法想像牠離開我的那一天。

Q5. What do you look like?

你的外觀如何？

參考答案：

What do I look like? I am tall and strong. I have square shoulders and good body shape. Because I am a PE teacher, I work out every day. Somebody says I look like a pop singer named Jay. But a big one.

我看起來如何? 我又高又壯。我有寬廣的肩膀與好的身材。因為我是位體育老師，所以我每天運動。有些人說我長得像一位流行歌手—— 周杰倫。但是是大一號的。

Q6. Do you like summer? Why or why not?

你喜歡夏天嗎？為何或為何不？

參考答案：

Yes, I like summer because the weather is better. In hot weather, I can do things like swimming and eating ice cream. Also, in summer, I'll have a long vacation, so I love it very much.

是的，我喜歡夏天，因為天氣比較好。在熱天氣裡，我可以做些如游泳和吃冰淇淋的事，同時在夏天我有一個長假，所以我喜歡夏天。

Q7. Your friend is on his way to 7-11. Ask him to buy something for you.

你的朋友在去 7-11 的途中。請他幫你買些東西。

參考答案：

Are you going to 7-11? I need you to buy something for me. I'll have picnic tomorrow, so I need some drinks and cookies. Help me grab something you like. I definitely like them, too. Thanks a lot.

你要去 **7-11** 嗎?我需要你幫我買一些東西。我明天要去旅遊野餐，所以我需要一些飲料與餅乾。請幫我抓一些你喜歡的東西，我也絕對會喜歡的。多謝。

TEST 2

第一部分：複誦

> 共 5 題。題目不印在試卷上，由耳機播出，每題播出兩次，兩次之
> 間大約有一至二秒的間隔。聽完兩次後，請馬上複誦一次。

1. Sam always has bananas for breakfast.
   得分關鍵：**has bananas for breakfast** 是「早餐吃香蕉」的意
   　　　　　思。

2. Is Bob a teacher or a secretary?
   得分關鍵：**secretary**是祕書的意思。

3. How does she go to school?
   得分關鍵：本句問「她如何去上班？」，疑問詞的問句語調下
   　　　　　降。

4. I didn't see you two days ago.
   得分關鍵：**two days ago** 是「兩天前」的意思。

5. His family comes from Italy.
   得分關鍵：**comes from** 是「來自」的意思，**Italy** 的重音在第一
   　　　　　音節。

第二部分：朗讀句子與短文

> 共有五個句子及一篇短文，請先利用 1 分鐘的時間閱讀試卷上的句子與短文，然後在 1 分鐘之內以正常的速度，清楚正確的朗讀一遍。

One : What kind of business does he have?

得分關鍵：**what kind of business** 是「什麼種類的事業」的意思，疑問詞的問句語調下降。

Two : Barney takes a bus to work every day.

得分關鍵：**takes a bus to work** 是「搭公車上班」的意思。

Three : You didn't do it, did you?

得分關鍵：附加問句 **did you** 的語調可以上升也可以下降。

Four : I go to the movies five times a week.

得分關鍵：**fives times a week** 是一週五次的意思。

Five : It's half past nine.

得分關鍵：**half past nine** 是 **9** 點過 **30** 分。

Six :

I often stay up for studying. I know it's not a good habit, but I am used to doing that. In order not to fall asleep, I always drink some black coffee in the late afternoon. My mother asks me not to drink so much coffee or tea because she thinks they are not good things for my body. Actually, I have tried several times, but I think it's impossible to quit my habits.

得分關鍵：“**stay up**”是「熬夜」的意思；而“**am used to**”則
是「習慣於」的意思。其中“**actually**”是個轉折詞，
在唸的時候可以做語氣的停頓。“**several times**”則是
「幾回」的意思。

第三部分：回答問題

> 共 7 題。題目不印在試卷上，由耳機播出，每題播出兩次，兩次之
> 間大約有一至二秒的間隔。聽完兩次後，請馬上回答，每題回答時間
> 為 15 秒，請在作答時間內儘量表達。

Q1. How do you feel when you see a rat?
當你見到老鼠時會覺得怎樣？
參考答案：
**I feel very scared when I see a rat. I think I don't like rats at
all. They are really terrible animals in the world.**
當我見到老鼠時會覺得非常害怕。我想我一點都不喜歡老鼠。
它們實在是世界上可怕的動物。

Q2. How is the weather today?
今天天氣如何？
參考答案：
**Today is a beautiful day. The sun is shining and the wind is
breezing. I like this kind of weather so much.**
今天是個美麗的日子。陽光普照，微風輕吹。我非常喜歡這樣
的天氣。

Q3. Do you like coffee? Why or why not?

你喜歡咖啡嗎？為何或為何不？

參考答案：

Yes, I like coffee so much. I drink coffee every afternoon, and I think I always feel relaxed and comfortable after drinking a cup of coffee.

是的，我非常喜歡咖啡。我每天下午都喝咖啡，而且我覺得在我喝了咖啡之後，我總是感覺放鬆與舒服。

Q4. How long does it take from your home to your school or office?

從你家到學校或公司要花多少時間？

參考答案：

It takes me over one hour from my home to my school. It's really the hard work for me. Because my first class starts at 8:00, I have to get up very early every day.

它要花我超過 1 個小時的時間從我家到學校。這對我來說實在是個辛苦的工作。因為我的第一堂課早上8點開始，所以我每天都要非常早起。

Q5. How far is it from your home to your school or office?

你家到學校或公司是多遠？

參考答案：

Actually I have no ideas how far it is. Yet, I know I have to take a bus ride for 30 minutes. It's OK for me.

事實上我對多遠沒有概念。但是我知道我需要 30 分鐘的公車車程。但對我來說還好。

Q6. Why do you want to pass the GEPT exam?

你為何想要通過全民英檢的考試？

參考答案：

My mother asked me to do that. She said that GEPT was a

useful and important test, so that I should pass it within one or two years.

我母親要我如此做的。她說 GEPT 是一項有用且重要的考試，所以我應該在一、兩年通過它。

Q7. You need a free ride to the airport. Call your friend and ask him or her to give you a ride.

你需要搭便車到機場去。打電話給你的朋友，要他或她載你一程。

參考答案：

Hi, could you give me a free ride to the airport? I need a car today but my father can't lend me his because he has to use it as well. But I have told my girlfriend that I would meet her then.

嗨！你可以載我一程去機場嗎？我今天需要車，但我父親今天也要用車所以不能借我。但我已經和女友說我會去接她。

第一部分：複誦

共 5 題。題目不印在試卷上，由耳機播出，每題播出兩次，兩次之間大約有一至二秒的間隔。聽完兩次後，請馬上複誦一次。

1. Two and two make four.
   得分關鍵：**make** 發【e】的長音。

2. I'll be more careful next time.
   得分關鍵：**I'll** 不要分成 **I will** 來唸。

3. We will be meeting twice a week from next month.
   得分關鍵：**twice a week** 是一週二次的意思。

4. We would like to exchange this swimsuit.
   得分關鍵：**exchange** 的 **a** 發長音【e】。

5. When will you graduate?
   得分關鍵：**graduate** 是畢業的意思。疑問詞的問句語調不要向上提。

第二部分：朗讀句子與短文

> 共有五個句子及一篇短文，請先利用 1 分鐘的時間閱讀試卷上的句子與短文，然後在 1 分鐘之內以正常的速度，清楚正確的朗讀一遍。

One：They are happy when they talk to each other.

得分關鍵：**They are happy** 是主要句，而 **when they talk to each other** 是時間子句。唸 **when** 時可以稍做停頓。**each other** 中的 **each** 發長音【i】。

Two：He promised that he wouldn't lie to her again.

得分關鍵：**promise** 的 **o** 發【a】的音。**wouldn't** 不要分開唸 **would not**。

Three：She told him not to mention the letter again.

得分關鍵：**mention** 是提及的意思。**not to** 可以稍做強調。

Four：He wanted to know if she was still angry with him.

得分關鍵：**want to know if ... .** 是想知道是否……。的意思。其中 **wanted** 的 **ed** 要發【ɪd】的音。

Five：She refused to listen to his excuses.

得分關鍵：**refuse to** 是婉拒的意思。

Six：

My mother is a good mother. She is the person who has influenced me for more than twenty five years. She is a beautiful woman, and she always teaches me lots of things, including some principles of what is good and what is bad.

得分關鍵：**twenty** 不要和 **twelve** 搞混。**influence** 是影響的意思。要多練習唸這個字。**principles** 是原則的意思。**including** 則是包括的意思。

第三部分：回答問題

> 共 7 題。題目不印在試卷上，由耳機播出，每題播出兩次，兩次之間大約有一至二秒的間隔。聽完兩次後，請馬上回答，每題回答時間為 15 秒，請在作答時間內儘量表達。

Q1. Where do you usually go for a walk?
你通常去哪裡散步？
參考答案：
I usually go for walk in a beautiful park in my neighborhood.
我通常在我鄰近地區的一個美麗公園散步。

Q2. What are you wearing today?
你今天穿什麼？
參考答案：
I am wearing a pullover and pants today.
我今天穿套頭毛衣與長褲。

Q3. When is your mother's birthday?
你母親生日是在何時？
參考答案：
Let's see. My mother's birthday is on May 21.
讓我想一下。我的母親的生日是5月21日。

Q4. Have you ever had a blind date?

你有相親過嗎？

參考答案：

Yes, my parents have arranged it for me once.

是的，我父母曾經替我安排一次。

Q5. Have you ever been on TV?

你有無上過電視？

參考答案：

Yes, once I attended a game show.

是的，有一次我上遊戲節目。

Q6. What is the best way to get news?

獲得新聞的最好方式是？

參考答案：

I think surfing on the line is the best way to get news.

我認為上網是最好的方式得到新聞。

Q7. Your friend is on his way to a drugstore. Ask him to buy something for you.

你的朋友在去藥局的路上。請你的朋友替你買些東西。

參考答案：

Are you on the way to the drugstore? I have a terrible headache. I really need some pain killers. Please get some pills for me. Thanks.

你正要去藥局的路上嗎？我有嚴重的頭痛。我真的需要一些止痛藥。請幫我買一些止痛藥。謝謝。

第一部分:複誦

共 5 題。題目不印在試卷上,由耳機播出,每題播出兩次,兩次之間大約有一至二秒的間隔。聽完兩次後,請馬上複誦一次。

1. He is building a model airplane.
   得分關鍵:**building** 要發 **ing** 的音要唸出。**model** 的 **o** 發【a】的音。

2. Maybe the show was cancelled.
   得分關鍵:**was cancelled** 是被動語態。**ed** 要發音。

3. The sign is about movie tickets.
   得分關鍵:**tickets** 是複數。

4. Why are you so mean to your parents?
   得分關鍵:可以特別強調 **mean**,有些責備的涵義在內。

5. Going to movies is my favorite hobby.
   得分關鍵:**favorite** 是最喜愛的意思,要多練習其唸法。**hobby** 發【a】的音。

第二部分：朗讀句子與短文

共有五個句子及一篇短文，請先利用 1 分鐘的時間閱讀試卷上的句子與短文，然後在 1 分鐘之內以正常的速度，清楚正確的朗讀一遍。

One : I accidentally hurt myself when I was cutting the vegetables.
得分關鍵：**accidentally** 是不小心的意思。**hurt** 的 **ur** 要發捲舌重音。

Two : They usually do their laundry by themselves once a while.
得分關鍵：**do their laundry** 是洗衣服的意思。**themselves** 要發【vz】的音。

Three : I can't start my car because there is not any gas in the fuel tank.
得分關鍵：**fuel tank** 是油箱的意思。

Four : Bird watching can be done on foot, or even in your own backyard.
得分關鍵：**done** 是個過去分詞，不可唸成 **do** 或是 **did**。唸 **even** 時可以稍做大聲強調。

Five : A balanced diet and reducing stress can all lead to a healthier heart.
得分關鍵：**diet** 與 **stress** 兩個字要多加練習其發音。**healthier** 是一比較級，必須清楚唸出它的尾音。

Six :
I came to the U.S. only two weeks ago. However, I miss my family very much because I lived with them for thirty years already. I also miss Taiwanese food, especially for " smelly tofu". I miss the beautiful weather in Taiwan as well. I hope to like the U.S. after I live here a long time.

得分關鍵：**However** 是轉折詞，朗誦時要稍做語氣的停頓。**smelly tofu** 是臭豆腐的意思。**as well** 則是「也是」的意思。

第三部分：回答問題

共 7 題。題目不印在試卷上，由耳機播出，每題播出兩次，兩次之間大約有一至二秒的間隔。聽完兩次後，請馬上回答，每題回答時間為 15 秒，請在作答時間內儘量表達。

Q1. Besides playing sports, do you do any exercises?
除了球類，你會做任何其他的運動嗎？
參考答案：
I always do aerobic in the gym.
我在健身中心做有氧運動。

Q2. Did you ever fail a test?
你有無曾經考試失敗呢？
參考答案：
Never, I always study very hard. I never failed a test before.
從未，我總是用功讀書。我從未考試失敗。

Q3. What's a good kind of book to read during a trip?
在旅行途中的好書是？
參考答案：
Magazines about entertainment are the best to read during the trips.
有關娛樂雜誌是旅遊期間最好的讀物。

Q4. Are you reading now?

你現在正在閱讀嗎?

參考答案:

Yes, I am reading Bill Clinton's autobiography.

是的,我現在在讀柯林頓的自傳。

Q5. What is something you shouldn't do when you eat?

什麼事情是你吃飯時不可以做的?

參考答案:

I shouldn't make strange noise when I eat soup.

我在喝湯時不可以出聲。

Q6. Do you have a big generation gap between you and your grandparents?

在你與你祖父母之間有無嚴重代溝呢?

參考答案:

Yes, I think so. Every time I talk to my grandparents, they always can't understand me.

是的,我這麼認為。每次我向我祖父母說話時,他們總是不了解我。

Q7. Your friend is on his way to a post office. Ask him to buy something for you.

你的朋友正在去郵局的路上。請他替你買些東西。

參考答案:

Hey, I need some stamps and envelopes. Would you be kind enough to get some for me when you go to the post office? Thanks a lot.

嘿!我需要郵票與信封。你可否幫我買些當你到郵局時?多謝。

第一部分：複誦

共 5 題。題目不印在試卷上，由耳機播出，每題播出兩次，兩次之間大約有一至二秒的間隔。聽完兩次後，請馬上複誦一次。

1. I enjoyed walking alone in the park in my free time.
   得分關鍵：**alone** 是獨自一人的意思。**free** 的 **ee** 發長音【i】。

2. I have a lot of fun swimming.
   得分關鍵：**swimming** 的尾音要明顯。

3. To become a superstar is my dream.
   得分關鍵：**dream** 的 **ea** 發長音【i】。

4. I go to hospital to see my dentist every three month.
   得分關鍵：**dentist** 是牙醫的意思。**every three month** 是每 3 個月的意思。在唸 **three** 時注意要將舌頭伸出發音。

5. To grade all these papers by 7:00 will be impossible.
   得分關鍵：**grade** 是批改的意思，其中 **a** 發長音【e】，**impossible** 要強調重讀。

第二部分：朗讀句子與短文

共有五個句子及一篇短文，請先利用 1 分鐘的時間閱讀試卷上的句子與短文，然後在 1 分鐘之內以正常的速度，清楚正確的朗讀一遍。

One：The younger children miss school more often than other children.
得分關鍵：**younger** 的 **er** 要有捲舌輕音。**children** 與 **child** 的發音不同要注意。

Two：We talked to Charles at the party, but neither of us liked him.
得分關鍵：**neither of** 是兩者皆非的意思。

Three：I dumped my boyfriend because he only talked about himself.
得分關鍵：**dump** 是拋棄的意思，要多練習。**himself** 的尾音要唸出來。

Four：My husband drove over his bike in the driveway by accident.
得分關鍵：**by accident** 是不小心的意思。

Five：All men's haircut are 10% off, even you pay by credit card.
得分關鍵：**10%** 要唸 **ten percent**。**credit card** 是信用卡的意思。

Six：
It is easy to learn how to make spaghetti. First, put some water, salt and oil in a pan. Then, put the pan on the stove for about fifteen minutes. After this, put the spaghetti into the pan for another ten minutes. After that, put tomato juice, oil, salt and meat in, and serve it with cheese finally.
得分關鍵：**spaghetti** 是義大利麵的意思。唸完轉折詞 **first**、**then**、**after that**、**after this** 後要做停頓。

Q1. Do you shake hands when you meet someone?
當你遇見人時會握手嗎？
參考答案：
Sometimes I shake my hands when I meet some people in a formal occasion.
有時在一些正式的場合中與人握手。

Q2. Where's the best place to make friends?
交朋友最佳場所是？
參考答案：
On the Net. I always make new friends through the Internet. A fitness center is also a good one.
上網。我總是在網路上結交新友人。健身中心也是一個好地方。

Q3. Who was your favorite teacher?
誰是你最喜歡的老師？
參考答案：
Charles. He is my favorite teacher in my language school.
Charles。他是我語言中心中最喜歡的老師。

Q4. Do you think there are too many holidays or not enough?
你認為假日太多還是不夠？
參考答案：
I think we have too many holidays in a year.
我認為一年中有太多的假日。

Q5. What is your lucky color?

你的幸運顏色是？

參考答案：

My lucky color is red. It is also a lucky color for Chinese people.

我的幸運色是紅色。它也是中國人的幸運色。

Q6. When do you usually have barbecues?

你通常何時烤肉？

參考答案：

I usually have barbecues on Mid-Autumn Festival.

我通常在中秋節時烤肉。

Q7. Your friend is on his way to the library. Ask him to borrow some books for you.

你的朋友在去圖書館的途中。要他替你借一些書。

參考答案：

Would you please borrow some comic books from the library? I want to spend my weekend on comic books. Thank you.

可否請你在圖書館替我借一些漫畫書？我想利用週末來看漫畫書。謝謝。

第一部分：複誦

共 5 題。題目不印在試卷上，由耳機播出，每題播出兩次，兩次之間大約有一至二秒的間隔。聽完兩次後，請馬上複誦一次。

1. I always go to my school by myself.
   得分關鍵：**by myself** 是獨自一人的意思。

2. Please come to me if you have any problems.
   得分關鍵：**Please** 的 **ea** 是發【i】的長音。

3. Your apartment seems bigger than mine.
   得分關鍵：**seem** 的 **ee** 是發【i】的長音。**bigger** 是比較級要將尾音清楚的唸出捲舌音。**mine** 則發出長音【aɪ】。

4. Tommy's grandfather plays golf every day.
   得分關鍵：**plays** 的 **s** 發【z】的音。

5. The hairdresser hurt her hand.
   得分關鍵：**hairdresser** 是美髮師的意思。

第二部分：朗讀句子與短文

> 共有五個句子及一篇短文，請先利用 1 分鐘的時間閱讀試卷上的句
> 子與短文，然後在 1 分鐘之內以正常的速度，清楚正確的朗讀一遍。

One：I am broke. I don't have any money in my bank account.
得分關鍵：**broke** 發【o】長音，**bank account** 是帳戶的意思。要
　　　　　多唸。

Two：The teacher always recovers from fatigue by going swimming。
得分關鍵：**recover** 是康復或恢復的意思。**fatigue** 中的 **gue** 發【g】
　　　　　的音，是疲勞的意思。

Three：My sister-in-law goes to the health club regularly to lose weight.
得分關鍵：**regularly** 是規律的意思。**lose weight** 則是減重的意思。

Four：Living in the dormitories saves students time and money.
得分關鍵：**dormitories** 是宿舍的意思。

Five：He quit working so that he could focus on his education.
得分關鍵：**focus on** 是專注的意思。而 **education** 是教育的意思。

Six：
Do you know something about color tests? A color test can tell you
about your personality. You pick up your favorite color, and then a
computer will tell you what kind of person you are. For instance, if
you like blue, you are a calm and faithful person. If you like red, it
means you are a romantic person.

第三部分：回答問題

共 7 題。題目不印在試卷上，由耳機播出，每題播出兩次，兩次之間大約有一至二秒的間隔。聽完兩次後，請馬上回答，每題回答時間為 15 秒，請在作答時間內儘量表達。

Q1. What appliances do you have at your home?
你的家裡有什麼電器設備？
參考答案：
I have lots of appliances, including fans, air-conditioners, and refrigerators, etc.
我有很多的家電設備，包括有電風扇、冷氣與冰箱等。

Q2. What's your address?
你的地址是？
參考答案：
My address is Park Road Number10.
我的地址是公園路 **10** 號。

Q3. Please describe your neighborhood.
請描述你的居家鄰近地區。
參考答案：
My neighborhood is a very convenient one. I can buy anything without driving in my neighborhood.
我的居住地區是非常方便的。我可以買任何東西而不用開車。

Q4. Did you work at 7-11 before?

你以前有在 7-11 工作過嗎？

參考答案：

Yes, but long time ago. It's a special experience.

是，但在很早以前。那是一個特別的經驗。

Q5. What kind of food is bad for you?

什麼樣的食物對你有害?

參考答案：

Sweet food and fried food is bad for me. I am easy to get fatter and fatter if I eat too much sweet and fried food.

甜食與油炸食物不好。我很容易就越變越胖假如吃太多的甜食與油炸食物。

Q6. How do you lose weight?

你如何減重?

參考答案：

I follow a special diet my doctor recommended.

我按照醫師給我的特別飲食建議。

Q7. Your friend is on his way to a grocery store. Ask him to buy something for you.

你的朋友在去雜貨店的路上。要他替你買一些東西。

參考答案：

I want to make some egg rolls for dinner tonight. Can you help me get some eggs and bean sprouts when going to the grocery store. Thanks very much.

我晚餐想要做一些蛋捲。當你去雜貨店時可否替我買一些雞蛋與綠豆芽？多謝。

第一部分：複誦

共 5 題。題目不印在試卷上，由耳機播出，每題播出兩次，兩次之間大約有一至二秒的間隔。聽完兩次後，請馬上複誦一次。

1. The man has to pay his bill.
   得分關鍵：**pay** 發【e】長音。**bill** 則發【ɪ】的短音。

2. The girl got her favorite dessert.
   得分關鍵：**dessert** 甜點與 **desert** 沙漠兩字重音不同，不可混淆。

3. His mom just ordered a snack.
   得分關鍵：**ordered** 是過去式，**snack** 唸時嘴要裂大，不可與 **snake** 混淆。

4. She is buying groceries.
   得分關鍵：**groceries** 是雜貨的意思。

5. The cashier is weighing the mushrooms.
   得分關鍵：**cashier** 要注意重音的位置，**mushroom** 發長音【u】。

第二部分：朗讀句子與短文

> 共有五個句子及一篇短文，請先利用 1 分鐘的時間閱讀試卷上的句子與短文，然後在 1 分鐘之內以正常的速度，清楚正確的朗讀一遍。

One : The president has lived in this city since 1996.
得分關鍵：**president** 總統，**present** 現在兩字要分別不可以混淆。**1996** 發 **nineteen ninety-six**。

Two : Each student has to work hard before taking the entrance exam.
得分關鍵：**each** 的 **ea** 發【i】長音， **entrance exam** 則是入學考的意思。

Three : There are many customers in the restaurant as the food is good.
得分關鍵：**customer** 的 **er** 要有捲舌輕音。**as** 在這裡當因為的意思。

Four : College education of this country has a lot of problems.
得分關鍵：**college education** 是大學教育的意思。**a lot of** 要唸清楚。

Five : News of her son's car accident was a terrible blow.
得分關鍵：唸 **accident** 時嘴要裂大。**blow** 是打擊的意思。

Six :
I have live alone in Taipei since I graduated from university. I miss my parents very much, yet I don't get many chances to go back home. Last night I heard a knock on the door. I opened the door and saw them standing outside. I was so touched with tears in my eyes.
得分關鍵：**graduated** 是畢業的意思 **ed** 要發出【ɪd】的音。**knock** 的 **k** 不發音。**touched** 則是感動的意思。

共 7 題。題目不印在試卷上，由耳機播出，每題播出兩次，兩次之間大約有一至二秒的間隔。聽完兩次後，請馬上回答，每題回答時間為 15 秒，請在作答時間內儘量表達。

Q1. Do you often buy your friends dinner?
你常請你朋友吃晚餐嗎？
參考答案：
That's impossible. I am just a student, and I have no spare money to offer someone's dinner.
那是不可能的。我是一個學生，而且我沒有多餘的錢可以請人吃飯。

Q2. Have you done something romantic before?
你以前有做過一些羅曼蒂克的事嗎？
參考答案：
Of course. I sent my girlfriends 999 flowers on her birthday.
當然，我在我女友生日時送她 999 朵花。

Q3. What's your biggest strength in language?
你在語言上的長處是？
參考答案：
I keep some new words in my mind I read before.
我記下我以前讀過的單字。

Q4. Are you afraid to see a dentist?
你害怕看牙醫嗎？
參考答案：
Yes , I am. I am afraid of seeing a dentist, even for a regular check up.
是，我是。我很害怕看牙醫，甚至是一般的檢查。

Q5. Do you take vitamins every day?

你每天吃維他命嗎？

參考答案：

Yes, I take vitamins every day because I think it is essential for my health.

是的，我每天吃維他命因為我覺得對健康是很必要的。

Q6. What is bad about living in a country?

住在鄉下的壞處是？

參考答案：

Boring. I can't go to KTV or MTV during the midnight.

無聊。在午夜時我無法去 KTV 或 MTV。

Q7. Your friend is on his way to a night market. Ask him to buy something for you.

你的朋友正要去夜市。請他幫你買一些東西。

參考答案：

Are you going to the night market? I need some night snacks and I miss "smelly tofu" so much. Please get some for me.

你正要去夜市嗎？我要一些宵夜而且我很想念臭豆腐。請幫我買一些。

第一部分：複誦

共 5 題。題目不印在試卷上，由耳機播出，每題播出兩次，兩次之
間大約有一至二秒的間隔。聽完兩次後，請馬上複誦一次。

1. One shopper is taking her change.
   得分關鍵：**shopper** 的 **er** 要有捲舌音，**change** 要發【e】。

2. The travelers found their luggage in the lobby.
   得分關鍵：**traveler** 的 **er** 要有捲舌音。**lobby** 的 **o** 發【o】的
   音。

3. There was much traffic on the highway last weekend.
   得分關鍵：**last weekend** 的 **t** 不發音。**traffic** 的 **a** 嘴要裂大。

4. I like living in the city.
   得分關鍵：**living** 要發出 **ing** 的聲音。

5. Amanda needs to make an urgent call.
   得分關鍵：**urgent** 要有 **ur** 的重音捲舌。**Needs** 則發【dz】的
   音。

第二部分：朗讀句子與短文

> 共有五個句子及一篇短文，請先利用 1 分鐘的時間閱讀試卷上的句
> 子與短文，然後在 1 分鐘之內以正常的速度，清楚正確的朗讀一遍。

One : I am to take a math course next semester.
得分關鍵：**semester** 是學期的意思。**math course** 的 **our** 要發捲舌
音。

Two : All members of the photography club need digital cameras.
得分關鍵：**photography** 是攝影的意思。**digital** 則是數位的意思。

Three : Your dress is really too fancy for the event.
得分關鍵：**too fancy** 要稍做強調音。**event** 的重音在第二音節。

Four : The music was so loud that it hurt my ears.
得分關鍵：**so loud** 要做強調音。**hurt** 的 **ur** 要重音捲舌。

Five : She traveled for three months in Australia last year.
得分關鍵：**three** 的音要注意。**Australia** 是澳洲的意思。

Six :
When I first came to the U.S., I was very homesick. I married my
husband one week before we came here. I left my wonderful family
and my successful career. Everyday when my husband went to the
university, I stayed in the apartment all by myself. I cleaned the
room and washed the clothes. Then, I always thought about my
family and friends. What a sad life!
得分關鍵：**first** 的 **ir** 是要有捲舌重音。**successful** 是成功的意
思。**What a sad life!** 有感傷的感覺。

共 7 題。題目不印在試卷上，由耳機播出，每題播出兩次，兩次之間大約有一至二秒的間隔。聽完兩次後，請馬上回答，每題回答時間為 15 秒，請在作答時間內儘量表達。

Q1. Do you ever buy used goods? What kind?

你會買二手貨嗎？什麼種類的？

參考答案：

Yes, I do. I have bought some used goods before. I've bought some used books and a used car.

是的。我以前買過一些二手貨。我有買過一些二手書與二手車。

Q2. What causes traffic accidents?

什麼造成了交通事故？

參考答案：

Careless drivers cause most traffic accidents.

粗心的駕駛造成大部分的交通事故。

Q3. Have you ever borrowed money from a loan shark?

你有曾經向地下錢莊借錢嗎？

參考答案：

Never. I always borrow money from my parents.

從未。我總是向我的父母借錢。

Q4. Are you an honest person?

你是一個誠實的人嗎？

參考答案：

Honestly speaking, I am not always an honest person.

老實說，我不總是一個誠實的人。

Q5. Do you think taxes are too high?

你認為稅太高了嗎？

參考答案：

Yes, my taxes are terribly high. I paid for 100,000 dollars this year.

是，我的稅太高了。我今年付了 **10** 萬元。

Q6. Are debates between candidates helpful?

候選人之間的辯論你覺得有用嗎？

參考答案：

Not at all. They are always arguing something that doesn't matter with me.

一點也不。他們總是爭執一些與我無關的事。

Q7. Your friend is on his way to a stationery store. Ask him to buy something for you.

你的朋友正在去文具店的路上。請他幫你買些東西。

參考答案：

If that doesn't bother you so much, would you please get some notebooks, pencils and rulers for me from the stationery store. Thanks very much.

假如不會太麻煩，請幫我在文具店買一些筆記本，鉛筆與尺。謝謝。

第一部分：複誦

共 5 題。題目不印在試卷上，由耳機播出，每題播出兩次，兩次之間大約有一至二秒的間隔。聽完兩次後，請馬上複誦一次。

1. I found the result as I had expected.
   得分關鍵：**result** 是結果的意思。**expected** 的 **ed** 過去式的音要發出來。

2. His friends kept him in the dark.
   得分關鍵：**kept** 是 **keep** 的過去式。**dark** 的 **ar** 要有捲舌音。

3. The issue is whether we can gain their support.
   得分關鍵：**whether** 是是否的意思。**gain** 中的 **ai** 發長音【e】。

4. The movie is on.
   得分關鍵：強調 **on** 一字。

5. The music is touching.
   得分關鍵：強調 **touching** 表示感人的意思。

第二部分：朗讀句子與短文

> 共有五個句子及一篇短文，請先利用 1 分鐘的時間閱讀試卷上的句子與短文，然後在 1 分鐘之內以正常的速度，清楚正確的朗讀一遍。

One : As a child, I would spend all day with my tutor.
得分關鍵：**tutor** 是家教的意思。其中 **u** 發長音【**ju**】。

Two : Jenny phoned him when he was watching TV.
得分關鍵：**Jenny phoned him** 是主要子句。而 **when he was watching TV** 是時間子句。

Three : She had never seen a book before she went to school.
得分關鍵：強調 **never** 表示從未之意。

Four : We pointed out that he had made some mistakes.
得分關鍵：**pointed** 的 **ed** 要發聲。**made** 則發長音【**e**】。

Five : I shall communicate with him more frequently in the future.
得分關鍵：**shall** 不同於 **should** 的唸法。**frequently** 是經常的意思。

Six :
I was having trouble adjusting to the weather in Chicago. When I went out for food shopping, my fingers and ears were freezing. Although I tried hard to get used to this kind of cold weather, I still failed to overcome it. In the end, I decided to leave for Los Vegas for a warmer weather.
得分關鍵：**adjusting** 是調整的意思。**Chicago** 芝加哥與 **Los Vegas** 拉斯維加斯兩地名要注意發音。**freezing** 中 **ee** 發【**i**】的音。**get used to** 是習慣於的意思，而 **fail to** 則是失敗的意思。**in the end** 唸完後語氣停頓。

第三部分：回答問題

Q1. How often do you go to the museum?
你多常去博物館？
參考答案：
Seldom. I don't like visiting museums.
很少。我不喜歡去博物館。

Q2. Do you understand art?
你對藝術了解嗎？
參考答案：
A little bit. Actually, I am interested in oil painting.
一點點。事實上，我對油畫很感興趣。

Q3. Do you think we will have enough natural resources in the future?
你認為在未來我們有足夠的自然資源嗎？
參考答案：
Certainly not. People in the world waste too many natural resources, so that we won't have enough ones.
當然不。人們總是浪費太多的自然資源，所以我們不會有足夠的資源。

Q4. Will we all speak the same language in the future?
在未來我們會說相同的語言嗎？
參考答案：
Probably not. There are too many races in the world.
可能不會。在世界上有太多不同的人種。

Q5. Do you like to take a bus? Why or why not?

你喜歡搭公車嗎？為何或為何不？

參考答案：

No, I don't because buses always crowed and slow.

不，因為公車總是擁擠而且很慢。

Q6. Do you buy any souvenirs when you travel overseas?

當你海外旅遊時，你會買紀念品嗎？

參考答案：

Yes, sometimes. However, I always don't know what to buy.

是，有時。然而，我總是不知要買什麼。

Q7. Your friend is on his way to a hardware store. Ask him to buy something for you.

你的朋友正在去五金行的路上。請他替你買一些東西。

參考答案：

I need a hammer and some nails to make a bookshelf for myself. I know you are going to the hardware store, so please do me a favor. Get them for me. I appreciate it.

我需要一把鐵鎚與一些鐵釘來為我自己做一個書架。我知道你正要去五金行，所以請幫我一個忙。幫我買他們。我十分感激。

第一部分：複誦

共 5 題。題目不印在試卷上，由耳機播出，每題播出兩次，兩次之間大約有一至二秒的間隔。聽完兩次後，請馬上複誦一次。

1. Experience is a good teacher.
   得分關鍵：**experience** 是經驗的意思。

2. The police are investigating the crime.
   得分關鍵：**investigating** 是偵察的意思。**crime** 則是犯罪的意思。

3. Rice is the staple food from the Chinese people.
   得分關鍵：**staple** 發【e】的音。

4. Neither of the two brothers can speak English.
   得分關鍵：**neither of** 是兩者皆非的意思。

5. We found the house empty.
   得分關鍵：**empty** 的 y 發短音【ɪ】。

第二部分：朗讀句子與短文

> 共有五個句子及一篇短文，請先利用 1 分鐘的時間閱讀試卷上的句
> 子與短文，然後在 1 分鐘之內以正常的速度，清楚正確的朗讀一遍。

One : Flowers are blooming.

得分關鍵：**blooming** 是盛開的意思。

Two : The police crack down on a call-girl station.

得分關鍵：**crack down** 的 **crack** 音嘴要裂大。**call-girl station** 則
是應召站的意思。

Three : I read the newspaper for my father.

得分關鍵：**newspaper** 發【e】的音。

Four : The doctor pronounced the man died.

得分關鍵：**pronounce** 是宣稱的意思。

Five : She watched me doing the work.

得分關鍵：**work** 中 **or** 要發捲舌重音。

Six :

Studying English takes time and patience, but it is definitely
rewarding. People use English everywhere, even for the e-mails. If
we can master English, that means we can be more competitive in
this international community.

得分關鍵：**patience** 是有耐心的意思。**definitely** 是絕對地。
rewarding 則是值得的意思。**competitive** 是有競爭力
的意思，重音在第二音節。**community** 是社區的意
思。**even for** 可以大聲做強調。

> 共 7 題。題目不印在試卷上，由耳機播出，每題播出兩次，兩次之間大約有一至二秒的間隔。聽完兩次後，請馬上回答，每題回答時間為 15 秒，請在作答時間內儘量表達。

Q1. What was your best vacation?
你最棒的假期是？
參考答案：
My best vacation was the one that I went to Bali island. It was so relaxing. I love it so much.
我最好的假期是到峇里島。這十分放鬆。我太愛它了。

Q2. What are the best places to visit in Taiwan?
在臺灣最棒的旅遊點是？
參考答案：
Kenting National Park and Taipei 101 building are the best place to visit because they are very special.
墾丁與臺北 101 是臺北最好觀光的地點，因為他們十分特別。

Q3. What is your favorite way to travel?
你最喜歡的旅遊方式是？
參考答案：
I like to fly around the world.
我喜歡坐飛機環遊世界。

Q4. Which countries have you visited?
你曾經去過哪些國家？
參考答案：
I have visited some countries, including Thailand, Japan, India and China.
我曾經去過一些國家，包括泰國、日本、印度與中國。

Q5. Did you ever have a bad experience during a vacation?

在旅遊期間有無不好的經驗？

參考答案：

Yes, I did. Once I lost my passport and that was really a terrible experience in my life.

是的。有一回我丟了我的護照，這是我人生中一個可怕的經驗。

Q6. Do you like rugby? Why or why not?

你喜歡英式橄欖球嗎？為何或為何不？

參考答案：

No, I don't like it. I don't understand it at all.

不，我不喜歡。我一點也不了解。

Q7. Your friend is on his way to a flower shop. Ask him to buy something for you.

你的朋友正在去花店的途中。請他替你買些東西。

參考答案：

Tomorrow is Valentine's Day. I know you are on your way to the flower shop nearby. Buy a bunch of roses for me. I want them for my new girlfriend. Thanks.

明天是情人節。我知道你正要去附近的花店。替我買一束玫瑰。我想要給我的女友。多謝。

附　錄

測驗項目

級數	初試	通過標準/滿分	複試	通過標準/滿分
初級	聽力測驗	80/120分	口說能力測驗	80/100分
	閱讀能力測驗	80/120分		
	寫作能力測驗	70/100分		
中級	聽力測驗	80/120分	寫作能力測驗	80/100分
	閱讀能力測驗	80/120分	口說能力測驗	80/100分
中高級	聽力測驗	80/120分	寫作能力測驗	80/100分
	閱讀能力測驗	80/120分	口說能力測驗	80/100分
高級	聽力測驗	80/120分	寫作能力測驗	三級/五級分
	閱讀能力測驗	80/120分	口說能力測驗	三級/五級分
優級	整合式寫作測驗	通過本級寫作測驗需在每個評分項目表現均達通過標準		
	整合式口說測驗	通過本級口說測驗需在每個評分項目表現均達通過標準		

全民英語能力分析檢定測驗

初級初試答案紙

聽　　力　　測　　驗		閱　讀　能　力　測　驗	
1 Ⓐ Ⓑ Ⓒ　　21 Ⓐ Ⓑ Ⓒ		1 Ⓐ Ⓑ Ⓒ Ⓓ　　21 Ⓐ Ⓑ Ⓒ Ⓓ	
2 Ⓐ Ⓑ Ⓒ　　22 Ⓐ Ⓑ Ⓒ		2 Ⓐ Ⓑ Ⓒ Ⓓ　　22 Ⓐ Ⓑ Ⓒ Ⓓ	
3 Ⓐ Ⓑ Ⓒ　　23 Ⓐ Ⓑ Ⓒ		3 Ⓐ Ⓑ Ⓒ Ⓓ　　23 Ⓐ Ⓑ Ⓒ Ⓓ	
4 Ⓐ Ⓑ Ⓒ　　24 Ⓐ Ⓑ Ⓒ		4 Ⓐ Ⓑ Ⓒ Ⓓ　　24 Ⓐ Ⓑ Ⓒ Ⓓ	
5 Ⓐ Ⓑ Ⓒ　　25 Ⓐ Ⓑ Ⓒ		5 Ⓐ Ⓑ Ⓒ Ⓓ　　25 Ⓐ Ⓑ Ⓒ Ⓓ	
6 Ⓐ Ⓑ Ⓒ　　26 Ⓐ Ⓑ Ⓒ		6 Ⓐ Ⓑ Ⓒ Ⓓ　　26 Ⓐ Ⓑ Ⓒ Ⓓ	
7 Ⓐ Ⓑ Ⓒ　　27 Ⓐ Ⓑ Ⓒ		7 Ⓐ Ⓑ Ⓒ Ⓓ　　27 Ⓐ Ⓑ Ⓒ Ⓓ	
8 Ⓐ Ⓑ Ⓒ　　28 Ⓐ Ⓑ Ⓒ		8 Ⓐ Ⓑ Ⓒ Ⓓ　　28 Ⓐ Ⓑ Ⓒ Ⓓ	
9 Ⓐ Ⓑ Ⓒ　　29 Ⓐ Ⓑ Ⓒ		9 Ⓐ Ⓑ Ⓒ Ⓓ　　29 Ⓐ Ⓑ Ⓒ Ⓓ	
10 Ⓐ Ⓑ Ⓒ　　30 Ⓐ Ⓑ Ⓒ		10 Ⓐ Ⓑ Ⓒ Ⓓ　　30 Ⓐ Ⓑ Ⓒ Ⓓ	
11 Ⓐ Ⓑ Ⓒ		11 Ⓐ Ⓑ Ⓒ Ⓓ　　31 Ⓐ Ⓑ Ⓒ Ⓓ	
12 Ⓐ Ⓑ Ⓒ		12 Ⓐ Ⓑ Ⓒ Ⓓ　　32 Ⓐ Ⓑ Ⓒ Ⓓ	
13 Ⓐ Ⓑ Ⓒ		13 Ⓐ Ⓑ Ⓒ Ⓓ　　33 Ⓐ Ⓑ Ⓒ Ⓓ	
14 Ⓐ Ⓑ Ⓒ		14 Ⓐ Ⓑ Ⓒ Ⓓ　　34 Ⓐ Ⓑ Ⓒ Ⓓ	
15 Ⓐ Ⓑ Ⓒ		15 Ⓐ Ⓑ Ⓒ Ⓓ　　35 Ⓐ Ⓑ Ⓒ Ⓓ	
16 Ⓐ Ⓑ Ⓒ		16 Ⓐ Ⓑ Ⓒ Ⓓ	
17 Ⓐ Ⓑ Ⓒ		17 Ⓐ Ⓑ Ⓒ Ⓓ	
18 Ⓐ Ⓑ Ⓒ		18 Ⓐ Ⓑ Ⓒ Ⓓ	
19 Ⓐ Ⓑ Ⓒ		19 Ⓐ Ⓑ Ⓒ Ⓓ	
20 Ⓐ Ⓑ Ⓒ		20 Ⓐ Ⓑ Ⓒ Ⓓ	

國家圖書館出版品預行編目資料

全民英檢初級保證班：聽力與口說（題
庫）／李淑娟 查爾斯 著.— 初版.— 臺
北市：書泉，2006[民95]
面； 公分.——（英檢保證班系列）
ISBN 978-986-121-261-6（平裝）

1.英國語言-問題集

805.189　　　　　　　　95005275

3AS6 英檢保證班系列

全民英檢初級保證班：
聽力與口說（題庫）

作　　　者 ― 李淑娟(87.3)　陳頎
發 行 人 ― 楊榮川
總 編 輯 ― 王翠華
主　　　編 ― 黃惠娟
責任編輯 ― 蔡佳伶
插　　　畫 ― 許權豪
美術編輯 ― 米栗設計工作室
出 版 者 ― 書泉出版社
地　　　址：106台北市大安區和平東路二段339號4樓
電　　　話：(02)2705-5066　傳　真：(02)2706-6100
網　　　址：http://www.wunan.com.tw
電子郵件：shuchuan@shuchuan.com.tw
劃撥帳號：01303853
戶　　　名：書泉出版社

經 銷 商：朝日文化
進退貨地址：新北市中和區橋安街15巷1號7樓
TEL：(02)2249-7714　FAX：(02)2249-8715

法 律 顧 問　林勝安律師事務所　林勝安律師

出 版 日 期　2006年4月 初版一刷
　　　　　　　2017年4月 初版六刷
定　　　價　新臺幣300元

行政院新聞局局版臺業字第1848號